MW01136016

Shattered
BEGINNINGS

no longer broken duet
book one

LILLY WILDE

Shattered Beginnings
No Longer Broken Duet: Book One
Copyright 2018 by Lilly Wilde

Cover Design: Cover Couture
Cover Photo: R + M Photography
Other Photo(s): depositphotos

This is a work of fiction. Names, characters, places and incidents either are the product of the author's imagination or are used fictitiously, and any resemblance to actual persons, living or dead, business establishments, events or locales is entirely coincidental. The author does not have any control over and does not assume any responsibility for third-party websites or their content.

All rights reserved. No part of this book may be reproduced, scanned, distributed, or transmitted in any form or by any means, including photocopying, recording, or other electronic or mechanical methods, without prior written permission of the author, except in the case of brief quotations embodied in critical reviews and certain other noncommercial uses permitted by copyright law.

Please do not participate in or encourage piracy of copyrighted materials in violation of the author's rights.

ISBN: 9781722283322

Books from
LILLY WILDE

A NOTE FROM LILLY

Dear Reader,

I hope you enjoy time in Branch and Ragan's world as much as I enjoyed creating it. While you're here, be sure to sign up for my newsletter to receive FREE books from your favorite authors, up-to-date information on my latest releases, featured authors, bloggers and other interesting tidbits.

DID YOU KNOW …
This book will be available in ebook, paperback, and audiobook editions at all major online retailers!
For up-to-date information, follow me on Facebook or visit my website.

REMEMBER …
When you've finished ***Shattered Beginnings***, check out the snippet of the sequel—***Salvaged Hearts***—included at the back of this book!

Happy Reading,
Lilly

PRAISE FOR LILLY

"As always, you weave a beautifully told story, even if it breaks my heart."

Amazon Reviewer

"The story is fraught with serious subject matter but handled so well that it flows from start to finish without pause. It's almost "experienced" more than it is read."

Amazon Reviewer

"This story is so beyond what I expected. It's so full of raw emotion and pain. I feel as though your writing is once again pulling me deeper into a story I may never recover from."

Amazon Reviewer

"It felt real and as a reader I was swept up into each moment as if I were there. My heart hurt, I was angry, and I felt the confusion, the hope, the pessimism—all of it. I am in awe of how realistic these characters are being portrayed. When it is ugly, they are allowed to be in that moment without a rush to make it all better, or half-baked excuses for the whys and hows of it all. Sometime life just sucks, it's hard, it's messy and you do the best you can—that is completely encompassed in these characters!! They feel real, like people you actually know and therefore can easily relate to."

Amazon Reviewer

Dedication

Thanks to the amazing young lady who trusted me with her story. Your strength and perseverance to break the cycle of abuse and neglect is truly an inspiration to us all.

Prologue

Branch

EVERYTHING MOVES AS IF IN SLOW MOTION—THE fifteen seconds ticking on the clock, the blue and white jerseys that race across the field, and the line that rushes to form a blockade for their most valuable player.

As the roar of the crowd falls into a hushed silence in the backdrop, the virile mix of humidity, sweat, and adrenaline urges me forward.

That's when I tell myself, *I've got this.* But then a break in my offensive line allows a 300-pound beast of testosterone to come barreling toward me.

In one fluid motion, I fake left and cast my gaze down the field.

I spot an opening.

I tighten my grip on the ball and hurl it forward.

My breath hitches as the football spirals toward the receiver.

He reaches for it, and then he's tumbling into the end zone, the pigskin tucked into his side. He rolls right and pops up, lifting the ball in the air.

The stadium erupts as the bodies of my teammates collide with mine.

I did it. Another record shattered.

My performance in the Pro Bowl has skyrocketed my position with the league.

This is what it's all about.

This is my life.

The only one I know.

The only one I want to know.

Chapter
ONE

Branch

January 5, 2017

THE PHONE RINGS.

I silence the call and drift back to sleep, only to be awakened moments later by a second chime. In my semiconsciousness, I recognize my brother's ringtone.

Instantly panicked, I answer.

"Yeah, what is it, Jace?" The rasp of sleep coats my voice.

"It's Mama."

For fuck's sake. "What's she done now?"

"She hasn't been home in four days and she's not answering her phone."

I sit up in bed, dread punching my gut. "Why didn't you call before now?"

"Because it was your game week."

"And?"

"You don't... you never... you're different on game weeks," he finally says, his voice small, almost as if he's afraid to say it.

I run a hand through my hair and try to figure out why the hell I ever trusted Mama with Jace again. "And you've been home alone all this time?"

"Yeah. I've been going to school and coming home after."

"Shit, you're eleven years old, Jace."

"I know how old I am."

"Watch it, kid. Don't get smart with me."

"I'm not getting smart, Branch. I'm just saying."

"If you're old enough to manage without adult supervision for four days, you're old enough to know you should have called before now."

"On the first day, I figured she'd gotten up early to run an errand or something," he says, still defending his position.

"And the days after?" My tone is sharp with misplaced anger I should be directing at someone else.

"I don't know."

"Did you call Dad?"

"No. Not like he's gonna show up anyways," he replies, his voice sad. "He always gives excuses, especially now that he has that new baby."

Yeah, he's probably right. Dad has been hit or miss for half of my life and for most of Jace's.

"Are you mad?" he asks.

"At you? No."

"At Mama?"

I'm pissed that he's concerned about something that a kid his age shouldn't be. "You don't need to worry about that. Just do what I say, and I'll be there later this afternoon."

"You're really coming home?"

The optimism in his voice reminds me that I've been a real putz of a brother. "Yeah. I said I was, didn't I?"

"Think you'll make it before school ends?"

His growing excitement for something as normal as spending time with his sibling kicks me where it hurts.

"You can come to my class and say hi to my friends. They'll go crazy!"

I grin. "I'll see what I can do."

"Try really hard, okay?"

That all depends on if I find Mama and in what condition I find her. I look at the time. "In case I can't get there until to-morrow, I'll call Jimmy and tell him to be on standby to pick you up after school. And you'll stay with him and Loretta until I get a flight out."

"Okay. The bus is here. See you later, Branch."

I press end on the call and let out a sigh. How the hell has he managed to fend for himself for four days? *Four fucking days.* Anything could've happened to him. I curse again, my train of thought lost as my eyes roam over the small lump in the bed beside me. My gaze lingers on the blond locks snaked from underneath the sheets.

Who the hell is she?

I reach over and pull her hair.

She doesn't move.

I pull again, this time a little harder. She finally turns over and lets out a deep moan as she looks up at me.

My brows scrunch as I fight to recall the details of the previous night.

I remember the face.

And the sex.

But not the name.

Not that it matters at this point. We'd done the deed, which means there's no longer a reason for her to be here.

"You need to go," I say and step out of bed.

She sits up, the sheet falling to reveal a rack I abused the night before. "What?" she asks, clearly caught off guard by my aloofness.

There's always an adrenaline rush surrounding the game, and last night's was on overload. Hell, it was the Pro Bowl, and although both teams were comprised of some great talent, all eyes were on me the second I stepped onto the field. Sports fans and fellow ballplayers alike wondered if I could live up to the hype. Not only did I live up to it, but I also walked away with the highest ranking of every player in the nation. Is there any wonder things went overboard? That I awoke with a woman whose name I can't remember? And now it's time to parlay my success. To fall back into my routine with my eyes focused on the prize, and although the blonde—even in her wake-up state—is beautiful and sexy as hell, she isn't the prize I want.

"You need to get dressed and go."

"Just like that?" Disbelief shades her tone as she rubs the sleep from her eyes.

I grimace, not sure why this is seemingly unclear. "Yup, just like that."

"Are you always so rude after you've gotten what you wanted?"

"Sugar, I'm pretty sure I was rude before I got it, so let's not pretend this is anything more than what it was."

She crosses her arms over her chest, her brow arched. "Oh? And what exactly was it?"

"An overzealous fan who wanted the opportunity to tell her friends she'd been in my bed."

"Are you kidding me? Fuck you."

"If I had time, I would, but I have someplace to be, so…" I trail off, gesturing toward the exit.

"And I thought my ex was a jerk."

I shrug. *Does she honestly think I want to hear this shit?*

She frowns and shakes her head. "Can I at least take a shower? I won't have time to drop by my place before work."

My instinct leans toward the negative, but a quick acknowledgment of my part in her predicament swings my decision. I gesture toward the bathroom. "Be my guest."

She slides from the bed, not bothering to cover up or grab her clothes. My eyes trace their way up her legs, admiring the tight curve of her ass as she steps away. Whatever her name is, her body is banging. And if I wasn't about to head out of town, I'd no doubt have her beneath me again for the next couple of hours. Yeah, I'd enjoy wiping that frown right off that pretty little face of hers.

While Blonde and Banging is in the shower, I step into the closet, bypassing row after row of clothes, expensive shit I've never touched, and a fully stocked bar to grab a packed duffel bag from one of the shelves. I then text my press agent Connie Wilson and tell her to get me on the next flight to Atlanta.

Still naked, I go to the kitchen and toss some greens, fruit, and protein into a blender and chug it down as I head back to the bedroom, my lips spread into a grin as I scroll my phone, scanning each headline about last night's game. As usual, "Branch McGuire—The Man on Fire," is trending. And talks of unprecedented contract deals are on every major sports news feed. I'm pretty sure my agent is already hammering out details with the general manager or with the owner himself. As for sports agents, Vaughn Fletcher's the best in the business, and he's the reason I have one of the largest iron-clad contracts on record.

A reminder pops up on my screen. My guest appearance on *Sports Center* the day after tomorrow. I press the speed dial for Connie, letting her know I need to cancel. Before we end the call, she manages to reschedule me for the week after.

Blonde and Banging is still in my bathroom. I scowl at the door, wondering what the hell is taking her so long and starting to regret I allowed her use of my shower. It prolongs her time here, rendering her a lingering annoyance. I don't do the *afters*—the goodbye hugs, the post-sex kisses, the after-fuck snuggling—none of that. She served her purpose and I gave her a night she'll never forget. That's all I signed up for. That's all I'll *ever* sign up for. The guys on the team coined it the Branch McGuire Sex Motto—*Fuck 'em and forget 'em*. I shake my head, laughing to myself at those assholes. Yeah, I'm a dick. And I know it, but it's the only way to protect the two things I hold sacred—football and my sanity.

Interview after interview, I'm asked if there's a special woman in my life. And year after year, the answer remains the same. *Yes, there is someone special. Mary McGuire, the woman who raised me.* As for anything beyond that... I'm not that guy. Not the one any woman should set her hopes on. Not the one any woman should dream of marrying. Not the one who will ride in on a white horse and save any damsel in distress.

Instead, I'm the exact opposite. I'm the guy who tells a woman that I'll never want a relationship. That all I want is to ravage the pink folds of muscle between her thighs. That I'm going to consume her body and walk away when I'm done. The one who'll tell her all the shameful, erotic pleasures she'll experience when I'm inside her because that's the shit she *really* wants to hear. Who'll satisfy those indecent desires she craves, even when she's too embarrassed to admit aloud that it's what she wants. That guy who will take control and invade every part of her body, make it purr for hours, and leave her sex swollen and aching with need long after I'm gone. Simply put… I'm the guy a woman will lust for but will never claim as her own.

No, I won't be single forever. I figure I'll settle down in a couple of decades. For now, one night is enough. I don't have the capacity to give anything more. Even now, knowing someone is in my space who isn't supposed to be is making me crankier than usual. I don't know how married guys do it. It's enough to make you cut your shit off. Well, maybe it's not *that* bad, but I don't see any bright sides to it.

Pushing down thoughts that serve no purpose, I move toward the bathroom as the blonde opens the door, watching as she drops her towel and pulls on her clothes.

My flight leaves a little before noon, giving me just enough time to shower, dress, and get to DFW International, so I really need to get her the fuck outta here.

"Thanks for an amazing night," she purrs, looking up at me and resting her gaze on my cock when she's reassembled.

Yeah, it's impressive. Even in its natural state.

I motion for her to follow me out.

At the door, she turns and says, "I'm sorry about earlier."

I smirk. *I'm sure you are.*

"I'd love to get together again sometime." She pulls her bottom lip into her mouth and her gaze trails over my naked frame. "You have my number, right?" she asks, when her eyes reach mine.

Is she serious? Like I'd really keep her fucking number? "I sure do, sugar," I lie. Why do women love hearing what they know isn't true? *I have your number all right. You're one of the many misguided who think they have what it takes to take me off the market.* That shit will never happen. I close the door behind her. Unless *Blonde and Banging* is her real name, she's just another one who's been fucked and forgotten... right along with her number.

Chapter
TWO

Ragan

April 14, 2008

"**G**ET OUT!" THE WORDS RING FROM MY stepmother with an ominous finality.

"I didn't do anything wrong," I shout back at her.

Cassidy takes a threatening step toward me, meeting me at eye level. "I said, get out." Her voice is a whisper that chills my skin. "I want you out of this house, *now*."

I look past her, staring at my father for support, but within the seconds my eyes connect with his, I know I have none.

I push past Cassidy and head to my bedroom. She wants me gone… I'm gone. *But where the hell will I go?* A sixteen-year-old high school kid with a part-time job, no family to speak of, and no car. Before I wrap my head around what's happening, Cassidy is on my heels.

"Put whatever shit you can in this bag and get the fuck out of here." She tosses a grocery tote on the bed.

I spin around and face the oppressor who is supposed to

be my caregiver… who is supposed to be my *mother*. "This is *our* house. Maybe you should be the one to pack *your* shit and go."

She flashes an evil grin that mirrors her soul. "Ask your father if he wants me to leave. Go ahead. I dare ya."

Sparring gazes communicate the answer to a question that needn't be voiced. We both know Dad will choose her. That he will *always* choose her. My eyes remain pinned on Cassidy, not seeing a person at all, but a monster. One who takes pleasure in my shame. One who gets off on my pain. How could God ever create such evil? And why is she hell-bent on unleashing every bit of it on me?

What did I ever do to her? Except hope she would one day grow to love me, or at the very least *like* me. I try to do everything exactly right. I have the highest grade point average in my class. All the teachers like me, and I get along with everyone. At home, I walk the line—I cook, I clean, I try to fit in and be what I think Cassidy wants me to be. I do as I'm told even when I know it isn't right—I do it. All because I want her acceptance… her love. I want a mom. That's all I've ever wanted. *A mom.*

But Cassidy never gave me a chance. She's never once shown me an inkling of love. She's only shown hate. From day one, she's cursed and degraded me. Turned my father against me. Beat me for the slightest of offenses—some that weren't mine to claim. And tonight, she's taking my family… and my home.

I hate her. With every fiber of my being, I hate her. For what she's *made* me feel, for what she *still* makes me feel— the degradation, the rage, the pain, the fear. All of it collides in my chest, each emotion crowding and overriding the other. Suddenly, they all come to a head, and my insides explode, releasing the last ten years of hatred I've harbored for the woman who's been nothing short of a tormentor to my brother Noah and me.

I tear toward her, my arms outstretched, and shove her against the wall. My hands are underneath her chin pressing against her windpipe. "I hate you," I whisper through gritted teeth. Fueled by the venom running through my veins, the intense throbbing blinds me of everything else. I only see what I feel… and I feel as though I could kill her.

"Da-vid." She shrieks Dad's name, but it comes out as garbled noise.

I press harder. "Not so tough without an extension cord, are you?"

She claws at my wrists and shifts my hands just enough. "David, help me!"

Within seconds, Dad rushes into the room and pulls us apart.

"Ragan!" His hands are on my shoulders, shaking me and ushering me away from his wife. "What are you doing?" he asks, his brows knit in confusion. "You need to calm down."

"*I* need to calm down? What about her? She's trying to kick me out of *my* home. Are you going to just stand by and let her?"

He looks back at Cassidy, holding the expectancy of her gaze for a long beat and finally turns toward me.

And his eyes say it all.

He's siding with her.

Again.

He opens his mouth, but I speak before he does. "Oh, shut up. I was stupid to hope you'd do the right thing for once and protect your own flesh and blood. That's never going to happen, is it?"

"Ragan—"

"Is it?" I demand, my voice an octave louder and sobs building in my throat.

I glare at him. It's as if he's mute, his mouth opening and closing, but words don't come. My vision blurs, tears jetting from my eyes as he takes a step back. I quickly swipe the back of my hand across my cheeks. But the tears still flow, and I let him see. I want him to know my cries aren't just for tonight. They're for *every* night. For *every* day he's failed me. They're for the anger and hatred I have for the woman who has rained down a decade of abuse on me and my baby brother. All while he—my *father*—sat back and let it happen.

"See that, David." Cassidy steps toward the two of us, one hand on her accosted throat, and pointing a finger at me with the other. "See how she talks to you? She has no respect for us."

I trigger a wad of saliva and spit in her face. "Fuck you, Cassidy."

She jumps back, her eyes wide and mouth agape.

Speaking my mind feeds a sense of liberation that's been cloaked with a hunger for her acceptance. I must have been out of my mind to have so desperately craved love and approval from an immoral reprobate like Cassidy Merritt. Besides, it doesn't matter what I do or say at this point. I'm being tossed out on my ass tonight. My dad's silence has pretty much confirmed that. So there isn't anything I can do to stop the inevitable.

I look up from the bag I'm stuffing with whatever I pull from my bureau and see my brother Noah and my stepsiblings watching yet another night that will be added to the book of family secrets.

"You have five minutes before I throw you out myself," Cassidy warns. She grabs my dad's hand, tugging him after her. To my dismay, he doesn't look back at me. Instead, he beckons my siblings to follow suit.

They all file from the room. All but the one who will be affected most by my departure. I look at Noah, and if my heart wasn't already shattered into a million pieces, it would most assuredly suffer irreparable breaks at this moment. Big doe tears stream from his eyes, his chest rising and falling with deep sobs. I worry more for him than I do for myself.

I only have minutes, seconds even, to wipe Noah's face and tell him the little things he should do to keep Cassidy happy. *Or as happy as can be for someone like her.* I do my best to still his trembling frame and offer him words of comfort. The same as always.

I look up to see Cassidy leaning against the doorframe.

"Tick. Tock." She folds her arms across her chest. "Time's up, you little bitch."

There it is. Her *nickname* for me. The name she's called me so often that I've learned to tune it out. But not tonight. Tonight it pulls on the last of my restraint. I take several calming breaths, reining in the urge to finish what I'd started earlier. *You can do this. For Noah, you can do this.*

With my gaze fixed on my brother, the knot in my stomach pulls tighter. Noah casts a nervous glance over his shoulder and looks back at me. His next words come as a shaky whisper. "I'll tell Cassidy the truth about the tissue. I'll stand up for you and confront our dad. Then you can stay."

I shake my head, signaling him to leave it alone.

Defending me will only make matters worse for him, so I make him promise to keep quiet. To think about himself.

Grabbing the tote and my backpack, I grasp my brother's hand and take the short steps down the hall to the living room. I scan the dimly lit space for my dad, but he's nowhere in sight. Why should I be surprised that even now he's somewhere hiding behind his cowardice?

Before Cassidy shuts the door in my face, I pull Noah into a goodbye hug and I walk away, knowing his silence and good behavior will never be enough to save him. Because my stepmother's triumph tonight isn't enough to fill that dark hole inside of her. Her demonic proclivities go deeper than that. She's lost control over me, so instead of celebrating her exploit, she's nursing her ire.

I think of how she's scarred my body... and my mind. And with me gone, Noah's next in line. I know from experience that for every scrap of anger she's holding, she'll use the belt, or something worse, to release it.

The blows will come hard and fast.

Across his naked behind.

One lash after the other.

Across his back.

His cries won't save him.

His welts won't faze her.

The broken skin won't make her stop.

She will keep going... until she's breathless.

I only pray his body can withstand what she has pent up inside her.

Chapter
THREE

Ragan

April 14, 2017

THAT WAS MY INTRODUCTION TO ADULTHOOD. NINE years ago to this day. I don't purposely keep track of it, but vivid recollections of that night crash into my thoughts every year around this time. Maybe because it happened the evening before my seventeenth birthday—the night I was facing my umpteenth beating from step-mommy dearest.

I'd committed the heinous crime of using Cassidy's *special* bathroom tissue—the two-ply she'd held under lock and key for herself and her kids. But it had been Noah who grabbed her private reserve, not me. When Cassidy snatched the extension cord from the wall and jerked Noah toward his bedroom, I'd known it would have been one of the worst beatings he'd ever suffer at her hands. I figured I could take it far better than he. So, I told Cassidy I'd done it—that it was me who'd gone to her locked cabinet and grabbed the lush roll of toilet paper. And my proclamation—though dishonest—was the only vindication she needed to turn that extension cord toward me.

But something inside me broke that night. I wouldn't accept the beating. I'd had enough. And when I grabbed the cord and yelled at her to stop, she'd had enough, too. She told me to get out. And without much of a choice, I did. That night, I walked away from a house I never wanted to see again. A house that was once my safe place. A house that became a sea of nightmares.

I was never invited back of course, not that I would have accepted. But when I finally had a car of my own, I *did* go back. Late at night, I'd drive by. But not for me. Never for me. It was for Noah. Wondering how he was being treated. Wanting to take him away from it all but knowing I wouldn't be able to.

Despite the unknown and the utter desolation of that night, it was probably still one of the best nights of my existence. Because it pushed me into a better life. And I shudder to think what would have become of me had it not been for *that* night… and for Patty Wade.

Patty had been my music teacher throughout high school, and my acceleration in her class was an affirmation of her talent as an educator. She'd taken a keen interest in me, and to her credit, I play six different instruments. She'd brought me into her home that fateful night and assured me I could stay as long as I needed, which was a good thing, because she was my only option.

My dad's family was somewhere in Indiana. And when Mom abandoned us, her family eventually stopped coming around. So I had no idea how to find them either.

I'd attempted a discreet plea for help once… when I found my uncle on Facebook. I sent a message, telling him we needed him. But he never replied. That's when I accepted that my brother and I were on our own. That no one was coming for us. That no one would save us. And no one did.

Patty had figured early on that something wasn't right at my house. I never confirmed her suspicions until the night I moved in with her. Her first instinct was to report the abuse, but then I remembered Cassidy's threats. She'd convinced us that we'd be sent to a foster family who'd treat us ten times worse than she ever did. So that's what bartered my silence—fear. And that fear is what made me lie to Patty, telling her that I was the only one Cassidy abused. That she'd never laid a hand on Noah or her own kids.

It was a carefully orchestrated fabrication. One where the abuse had only occurred twice. One where the process of rec-ollecting the details for the authorities would yield more trauma than the abuse itself. Evidently my story was convincing because she didn't report Cassidy. Or maybe Patty knew I was lying, but she understood I had a reason to. Either way, to this day, Patty remained a friend and savior.

I'd returned to school the following day as I had any other day, pretending everything was okay, giving off an air of being like everyone else—a normal high school kid with typical high school problems.

I'd always looked forward to school—the one place I could release the constant knot in my gut and simply be. Without worry of persecution. Without guilt for being myself. And thanks to Patty, I no longer flinched at the sound of the last bell, which signaled it was time to go home.

Because *home* was no longer a dirty word.

And my breathing was no longer constricted by fear.

The nightmare was finally over.

Or so I'd thought.

Chapter
FOUR

Branch

January 5, 2017

"IT'S GOOD TO SEE YA, BRANCH." JIMMY grabs my hand, pulls me in for a bro hug, and slaps me on the back.

"You saw me last month."

"Yeah, for all of twenty minutes after your game."

I shrug. "You know how it is, Jim."

"I get it. I get it. Everyone wants a piece of *The Man on Fire*. Best to give it to 'em while you can."

I cast a cautious glance over my shoulder then grab the Redhorns hat from the side of my bag. "Not so loud." I slide the cap on and pull the bill down low over my eyes.

Jimmy lifts a brow. "Don't want anyone to know you're here?"

"Nope."

"In that case, *todos quieren una pieza del hombre en llamas*," he repeats in his native language.

We exchange grins and head for the parking garage.

Except for a few curious glances, we make it to the car sans conspicuous whispers, endless selfies, or obligatory autographs. I toss my duffel into the back seat. "Thanks for picking me up."

"No problem at all. You know that."

In all the years I've known Jimmy Perez, he's never once let me down. In fact, he's been the most reliable person in my life. Always had my back. Looked out for me. But his concern came at a price. His friendship with my dad. Their relationship—which spanned thirty years, two marriages, and four kids—became one of scorned silence and distance.

Jimmy's a stand-up guy—good husband, breadwinner, and great father. While my dad, on the other hand, is an undependable, cheating louse. Jimmy gave him hell about it one too many times and they came to blows. That was seventeen years ago. They haven't spoken since.

He looks to the side, checking his blind spot, then pulls into the Hartsfield International Airport traffic.

I broach the reason for my trip. "Any word on Mama?"

"Nah, I called Denver and he's still checking the hospitals and shelters."

Denver Ruffin is the local sheriff, a friend from high school who's actually more like family. But in Blue Ridge, everyone's regarded like that in one way or another. Even me, the guy who hates to step foot in that town.

I pull my phone from my pocket and scroll the call history. "I've been trying Mama since this morning. Every call goes to voicemail."

I see the concern flash over Jimmy's features as he accelerates and merges onto the interstate. "We'll find her. Don't worry."

"It's hard not to worry about someone who can slip into an episode at any given moment," I murmur, more to myself than to Jimmy.

Mama has paranoid schizophrenia, a condition that went undiagnosed for years. Hell, I'd thought she was just crazy half the time. Had it not been for the league and the psychological battery they pushed us through, I'd still think it was a case of a woman who became slightly psychotic when her manipulative tactics failed. Because that's when it tended to manifest—when she wasn't getting her way.

After the psych tests, the players were given a shitload of mental health pamphlets. Some were undoubtedly intended for the wives. Being the wife of a pro athlete is a mental breakdown waiting to happen. Why either party would subject themselves to such hell is beyond me.

In skimming the leaflets, one caused my hair to stand on end—it was a fact sheet that ticked off everything I'd come to recognize as Mary McGuire. Knowing it wouldn't be an easy sell, I approached her with my speculation. As expected, she was enraged by the possibility and even more so that I thought she had a mental condition. She avoided my calls for days, and when I returned to Blue Ridge to push the issue, she gave me the silent treatment. Over the years, I'd learned that threats and guilt trips were the only ways to get her to see reason at times. That's why I played the ultimate card—I threatened to take Jace, and my "heartless tactic"—as she called it—is what finally forced her to undergo a psych evaluation.

As it turned out, I was right. I didn't know if that gave me more cause for worry or less, but at any rate, her unnatural behavior finally had a name. And after a period of Dr. Blake's combination therapy, Mama's behavior became recognizable... and consistent. Although I doubted she'd ever be the person she once was, Blake's reports were favorable and afforded me the comfort to leave Jace in her care. But now I'm kicking my ass for thinking I could trust her to stay on track.

Jimmy interrupts my thoughts. "Folks will be excited to see you a month earlier than usual."

I grimace. "Maybe. Maybe not."

"When are they ever *not* excited when you step inside our city limits?"

"Let's just say I plan to step in and step out *unnoticed*."

He frowns, his eyes cutting to mine. "One of these days, you're gonna have to let go of that past stuff, Branch. No matter where football takes you, Blue Ridge is home."

I nod. I don't agree, but it's not a discussion I plan to have. Home should inspire *some* sense of comfort, not the familiar edge of bitterness that creeps in with each mile that brings me closer to Blue Ridge.

My trips to Georgia have been reduced to *have-tos* and the annual charity the city hosts in my honor. I suppose I don't mind *that* trip. It's the ones like this that piss me off— the ones I *have* to take.

I let out a huff, recalling the last time I had to come home to find Mama. It was two years ago. She and Jace were flying out to Dallas for a visit, but at the last minute, Mama backed out. The change of plans didn't lessen Jace's excitement, but Mama wouldn't let him be. She'd called him every morning, asking when he was coming home. She refused to speak to me at all, claiming I was making moves to take him away from her.

One particular morning, when Jace and I were headed to

the Frisco practice facility, she called with some off-the-wall commentary Jace didn't quite understand, so he passed the phone to me. Annoyed, I asked why she couldn't let the boy enjoy his school break. She shifted gears, insisting she had to go because *they* were calling her name. Clueless as to her whereabouts or her inference, I called back, but she didn't answer. Call. Voicemail. Call. Voicemail. The cycle went on for about an hour. The find-my-phone app indicated she was at the house, so I had Jimmy go by to check on her, but *she* wasn't there. Pissed that I had to cut Jace's trip short, we returned to Georgia. Three days later, Mama turned up at the bus station. She'd been there the entire time waiting to catch a bus to some town that didn't fucking exist.

Is my anger justified? Probably not. Her condition isn't her fault. But when she does things that place Jace in harm's way, it's hard to see her as the innocent, especially when I suspect she's missing again for the same reason as before... which from my perspective is very much her fault.

I stare at the road, cursing in my head until Jimmy brings me back from my thoughts. He keeps my mind occupied, briefing me on the latest in the small town of Blue Ridge. I swear he gossips more than his wife Loretta.

When he asks about life in Dallas, I tell him about the players, the locker room brawls, the parties—things he wouldn't see on TV or read in *any* magazine. I fill him in on my shit, too—the exploits, the indulgences, testing the elasticity of the cheerleaders, the night with the twins.

Jimmy is well aware of my inclinations for sex. And he knows that beyond fulfilling the need to get laid, I never plan to get close to any woman. Though he wants a different lifestyle for me, he doesn't judge. He just listens and gives the same drill—never lead a woman on and never go bareback. Beyond that, he grins and shakes his head at my stories.

"Man, that's some life, Branch. If I were a few years younger... and single, I'd have to move to Texas with ya."

"As if you could function without Loretta."

"True." He chuckles. "By the way, she's cooking dinner in your honor tonight, so we expect you at seven."

I shake my head, exhaling the worry in my chest. "Hope we find Mama by then."

"And if we don't, come anyway. You need to be with family."

"Thanks, Jim."

"Now don't go thanking me again. You know you're like the son I never had. Especially since my house is full of girls."

I glance at him, familiar with his paternal sentiment but thrown off by the weird grin spreading across his lips. "What's so funny?"

"Loretta's pregnant."

My brows shoot up. "No way!"

"Yep. Six months. We're hoping it's a boy this time."

"Man, I thought you were done having kids. Four is more than enough."

"Yeah, my wallet and my sanity can attest to that."

Jimmy always jokes about a houseful of hormonal girls because he knows it will get Loretta riled up, but I've never known a man more devoted to his family.

"It wasn't planned," he goes on. "Especially at her age. But doc says everything looks good. We're expecting Little Jimmy by the end of April."

"That's great, Jim. Congratulations. So you finally get your boy, huh?"

He winks at me and shoves my shoulder. "I'll get my *second* boy."

Although acknowledged, I rarely respond to Jimmy's familial expressions.

"We don't *really* know if it's a boy," he adds, redirecting his attention to the road. "Loretta wanted it to be a surprise, so we're waiting. I'm planning for a boy, though. I mean, what am I gonna do with five girls in the house?"

I chuckle and throw a glance his way. "The same thing you do with four."

When he stops for gas, he lowers the top of the convertible and we're soon back on I-85. That's the thing about Georgia weather; even near the dead of winter, it's still hot as hell. I shove my hat in the glove box and slip on my aviators. Twenty or so miles later, I recline my head on the seat and wonder in what condition I'll find Mama.

Sooner than I expect, we pull up to Jimmy's and out comes Loretta, her belly a couple feet in front of her.

I whisper to Jimmy, "Are you sure it ain't twins?"

He snickers and slides out of the car. "Don't let Loretta hear you say that."

"Hola, Branch," she says, waddling toward me. "Let me look at you. It's been too long. You need to come home more often. We miss seeing you around here."

"Now don't go bugging the boy about that, Loretta."

Although Jimmy agrees with his wife, he knows the frequency of my visits to Blue Ridge is a sore subject.

"Give me a hug and come on in," she says.

I let out a low whistle. "Damn, Loretta." I kiss her on the cheek and step back, her pregnant stomach keeping her at arm's length. "I didn't think a pregnant woman could look so fucking hot."

Jimmy nudges me and takes my place beside his wife. "Hey watch it, kid. You may be like a son, but that doesn't mean I won't kick your butt."

Loretta's a beautiful woman—a petite Latino goddess who's Jimmy's sole purpose for breathing. He's *warned* me about her a few times over the years. But it's all in fun. She only has eyes for him and she's more like a second mom to me.

"Aren't you coming in?" she asks when I don't move to follow her.

"He's here to find Mary," Jimmy says. "And he needs to check on Jace. They're coming back for dinner though."

"Good, because I'm making all your favorites," she says, still smiling at me.

Jimmy passes his hand over Loretta's stomach and crouches down in front of her. "How's my boy doing in there?"

She bats his hand. "Get away from me, Jimmy. We both know it's another girl."

"You hear that, Little Jimmy? *Tu madre te está llamando niña.* We're just gonna have to show her, aren't we?" He stands upright and pulls his wife into a hug and kisses her lips. When Jimmy releases her, she looks up at him as though the world starts and stops with him.

His girls are lucky—being raised by those two. Maybe if I'd grown up in the presence of that type of affection—even a fragment of it—I wouldn't avoid *home.* Or at least I wouldn't have to rush here to tend to messes that aren't mine to clean.

I clear my throat and they both look over at me. "I'm gonna head out. Jace wants me to drop by his class."

"He and his friends will get a real kick out of that," Jimmy says. "Not to mention, all the attention it'll bring his way."

"Yeah, I think that's the *real* reason he wants me there—the attention."

Loretta lifts a brow. "Wonder who he gets *that* from."

"Hey, I don't ask for it. Hell, most times I avoid it." *At least when it comes to Blue Ridge.*

"Well, you *are* a very handsome man, Branch. If I were younger and single… and if you weren't like a son to me, I'd—"

"You'd do nothing, Loretta. Nothing at all. So hush up the foolish talk and let the boy get on his way," Jimmy says.

Loretta winks at me, and Jimmy smacks a palm across her backside.

"You guys should be on a reality show." I chuckle at their exchange. "Ratings gold."

"Go ahead and we'll see you in a bit." He passes me his keys. "I'll make a few more calls and we can go to the police station when you get back."

"Thanks, Jim. Call if you hear anything."

I fold into his 1957 Chevy Corvette and head across town to Fannin County Middle School, pulling into the parking lot at least an hour before school lets out. Not much has changed since I walked the grounds of the school several years ago. I slip back in time, picturing the guys from the team waiting for me outside the principal's office. I was there as often as I was in class. I chuckle to myself and step into the main office.

The shapely Mrs. Harris has been replaced by a heavyset secretary with a heap of bright red hair piled atop her head. She looks up with an air of recognition followed by the starstruck eyes wide with disbelief.

"You're… Oh. My. God." Her hand clutches her chest.

"You're Branch McGuire! *The* Branch McGuire."

After a beat, I say, "That's the name on my license."

"Oh, my word," she exclaims and reaches for the phone, her eyes still pinned on me. The receiver falls to her desk and she glances down briefly to lift it then presses a button on the keypad. "Mr. Fowler, you should come out here. *Now.*"

"I'm here to see my brother. Do I need to sign something?"

Ignoring my question, she tears a slip of paper from her pad and pushes away from the desk. "My husband would kill me if I didn't get your autograph. Would you mind?"

"Is that Branch McGuire?"

I look up from the excited ginger to see Principal Fowler stepping from his office.

"You know." He shakes a finger at me as his lips curl upward. "I should have a detention room dedicated to you."

"I thought you had," I say, laughing with him.

"Good to see you, Branch." He shakes my hand. "Tonya, are you bugging him for an autograph?"

"Well, yes, sir."

Her eyes have yet to leave my face.

"And a selfie, if it's not too much trouble," she whispers, although Fowler is close enough to hear. "My girlfriends will simply die when they see it."

"You're right… they would, which is why it's not going to happen," Fowler says, his voice firm. "Now get back to your desk. The man isn't here to let you snap pictures to put on that darn Facebook or the Twitter. Trump does that enough for everybody."

I shrug one shoulder. "It's okay. One picture won't hurt."

Disregarding her boss, the ginger rushes to her purse for her cell and after snapping two photos, she's back at her desk, tapping on the phone screen, more than likely doing exactly what Fowler said she'd do. *So much for my plan to remain unnoticed.*

Minutes later, I'm strolling down the hall to Jace's last-period class. The door to Ms. Tucker's room is already open. She looks up when she notices someone watching, her eyes big as saucers when she recognizes *who* the someone is. Stumbling over herself, she beckons me to come in.

The class is a mix of gasps and whispers as Jace rushes to the front of the room to hug his big brother. "You're here. You're actually here!"

And there it is again—the euphoric sound in his voice that kicks me in the gut.

Chapter
FIVE

Ragan

April 15, 2008

T HE GUIDANCE COUNSELOR DECLARES MY 4.6 GPA guarantees acceptance to pretty much the university of my choice, and it probably does… if my plan were to pursue a college education, but it isn't. I never thought beyond high school graduation and freedom from Cassidy and Dad. With the latter resolved, I find myself either making up for lost time or coping with the guilt of leaving Noah behind.

I'm sitting in third period, chatting it up with my best friend Hayley when a message sounds over the intercom. It's Mrs. Waters. She's requested I come to the main office.

Strange.

I've only been summoned to the office when Cassidy…

I bring that train of thought to a halt, confident that Mrs. Waters's call is related to my impending graduation. Even so, my mind wanders, conjuring details of my last visit to the school office.

A visit that very much involved Cassidy.

She appeared under the guise of my forgotten research paper when her real intent was to drag me to the bathroom for one of our *talks*. Before leaving for school, I'd completed my morning chores, including cooking breakfast for the family and cleaning the kitchen afterward. But I'd been rushing to catch the bus, and in my haste, I'd failed to notice the bread crumbs on the counter nearest the stove. For that oversight, I'd be punished. And it wouldn't wait until after school. It would happen as soon as my stepmother could get her hands on me.

In the bathroom stall, Cassidy directed me to lower my pants and underwear. I did as I was told. And then I was warned not to cry. She next grabbed a wooden hairbrush from her purse and ordered me to bend over. And without pause, she started in on me, cracking the back of the brush over each bare cheek. Twenty strikes each. I remember the number vividly because she'd made me count—she always made me count. Each slap to my tender flesh incited an involuntary response to cry out. But I suffered in silence, squeezing my eyes tight, biting my lip, and riding through each blow.

When it was over, she told me to pull my pants up and to look at her. My eyes were dry and I was devoid of all emotion. For this setting, that's what she required. So that's what I gave. My body had conditioned itself to the abuse. So whereas a *normal* person would typically cry, my tear ducts knew not to betray me. And they didn't.

I stared at Cassidy and waited for her speech—the one where she threatened my brother and me if I ever told anyone.

"Next time, do as you're told. Do you hear me?"

"Yes."

Her palm lands solidly across my cheek. "Yes, what?"

I ignore the sting of her assault and reply the way she expects. "Yes, ma'am."

"You will keep that house clean and that includes wiping every kitchen counter. How many times must I tell you that, you disobedient little bitch?"

"I'm sorry. I didn't mean to skip that one. But the bus was—"

"Get back to class. And I'd better not get a call about you crying. If I do, you'll get far more than a measly hairbrush across your ass. Do you understand?"

"Yes, ma'am."

I returned to class that day as though nothing had happened. My expression impassive, my eyes dry. Cassidy didn't want anyone to know what she'd done, so I didn't dare expose my pain.

Not in public.

Never in public.

But at home, she required something different. She wanted each strike to elicit my suffering. She wanted to see that she was hurting me, breaking me. So at those times, I gave her the tears. I cried. Because if I didn't, the lashes were harder. Relentless. Wounding. I learned to create tears when I had none. To put on the show she needed. She wanted to see the hurt and fear in my eyes, so I'd forced myself to give her that—to give her the broken mess of a girl she wanted at her mercy.

I catch myself extracting another memory... and then another. Yet as quickly as I bring them to the surface, I smother them, not wanting to remember anymore. Wanting to forget. And after last night, I can. Cassidy and the depravity that surrounds her are behind me. *She will never hurt me again.*

When I step into the school's main office, it's with an assurance that everything will be fine. Mrs. Waters looks up with a kind smile. "Good morning, Ragan. Your mother's here," she says, motioning toward the small sitting area to my right.

The knot that's been absent suddenly pulls tight in my chest. I follow the secretary's gaze to find Cassidy sitting in a metal-framed chair, her legs crossed and a fake smile spreading over her wicked lips.

"There you are," she says. "Let's talk in the hall."

I walk over to Cassidy and whisper, "I'm not going anywhere with you." And for the first time, I know I don't have to.

She tilts her head to the side, and a malicious smile replaces the sweetness of the fake. "Are you forgetting that Noah is still in my house?" She leans forward and grants a whisper of her own, one that sends chills down my spine. "Do you want him to get something that's intended for you?"

Her subtlety isn't lost on me. I understand the implication. And since Cassidy isn't in the habit of making threats without following through, my brother will assuredly suffer. And her malevolence will be incomplete until she's furnished evidence. She'll make certain that I see what she's done—that she's left Noah's body battered and bruised. And she'll place the blame solely on me.

Cassidy stands and walks out of the office, expecting me to follow.

And I do.

To our usual rendezvous point.

The bathroom.

She kicks open each stall door, checking that we're alone. Then she turns toward me, staring.

I square my shoulders, crossing my arms over my chest. "What do you want, Cassidy?"

She walks toward me, stopping when we're a couple of feet apart. "Just reminding you to keep your mouth shut. You may be out of my house, but your brother isn't. So if you say anything, you know what will happen to him, don't you?"

I glare at her, wanting to rip her insides out.

Cassidy raises a hand at me and I flinch.

"Answer me," she barks.

"I won't say anything."

"Good." She lets out a breath. "We have an understanding then."

I don't respond. What can I say? She holds all the cards and she knows it.

"Well, that's all I wanted. Go back to class… or not. I could care less," she says, pulling the mop of brownish-gray hair to one side of her head. "You're no longer my problem." She starts toward the door and I follow, but she stops as her hand grips the handle. "And by the way, I packed up all of your crap and had David set it on the curb. If you want it, you'd better get it before the garbage man picks it up tomorrow."

"You're an evil piece of shit, Cassidy. There are no words for how much I hate you."

She tosses her head back with a bitter laugh. "You stupid little bitch. Do you honestly think I care? I'm so glad to have you out of my house."

My hands fist at my sides. *It's not your house, you stupid whore.* I should have choked the life from her miserable body the night before.

She smirks and walks out, leaving me staring after her.

I exhale the air in my lungs, releasing the anxiety she placed in my chest. And then, still too shaken to return to class, I decide to skip. *Not like anyone gives a fuck either way.* I step to the sink, splash water across my cheeks, and stare in the mirror. I replay Cassidy's words. From the first to the last. Even the part about Dad. He set my belongings on the curb. *My personal items. My drawings.* They're sitting there... outside. Waiting to be hauled off as garbage.

Tears spill from my eyes.

Why couldn't this all be a horrible, horrible dream? Why is it based in reality? And why is there no end in sight? Even nightmares offer *some* type of finality when your eyes flicker open or when the dream fades to a close. But not for me. The bad never stops. It's as if someone has pressed a recycle button that spits out shit on top of shit. No one deserves this life. No one should walk through each day with a constant ache in their heart. No one's dreams should only consist of running away from a family that doesn't bear the meaning of the word. And now, after more than a decade of abuse and dysfunction, I fear I'll never fully comprehend the meaning myself.

Another by-product of Cassidy, Dad, and... Mom.

I loathe Cassidy, and I loathe my father with equal measure. But most of all, I loathe my drug addict of a mother for running away. For not getting better. For leaving me behind when I was only four years old. For not being here to celebrate each milestone—to celebrate days like this one.

My birthday.

It will pass exactly like the others—uncelebrated and unnoticed. And like every year, I'll count the hours until the day is over. Until I can forget that no one cares. That I'm alone. That I don't know what unconditional love feels like. And that I probably never will.

Those are the cards I've been dealt.

I snap from my thoughts and frown at my appearance in the mirror.

I splash more water on my face, rinsing away the residue of my suffering. I tell myself that a pity party serves no purpose. So I rein in the positives.

I'm free of the cruelty and exploitation. I realize that truth. I embrace it.

I'm finally safe. I take a deep penetrating breath, bathing my insides with this acknowledgment.

But reality is lurking in the shadows. It seizes the pit of my gut and siphons every ounce of my composure.

Cassidy can still hurt me.

By hurting Noah.

And poof, just like that, it's gone. The fragility of my calm becomes apparent, and a sharp stab pierces my chest. Each breath is constricted. Each pull of air into my lungs is tainted with the horror of the past and the threat of the future.

I have no weapons for this fight. I've nothing but anguish and despair. And those are by no means the artillery needed to go up against Cassidy. So maybe karma will take on this one. Maybe karma will wrap its tendrils around Cassidy's throat and finish the job I started. But does karma even exist? I have to believe it does, so I'll hold on to it like it's the only thing I have… because it is.

I grab a paper towel and dot my face.

One of these days, Cassidy Merritt will get what's coming to her.

For now, I play by her rules.

Because I have no choice.

Because of the cards I've been dealt.

Because of my love for Noah.

Chapter
SIX

Branch

January 5, 2017

"I CAN'T BELIEVE YOU CAME," JACE SAYS, LOOKING UP, smiling between licks of chocolate ice cream.

I tousle his hair. "I told you I would, didn't I?"

"Yeah, but I figured you'd send Mr. Jimmy or Miss Loretta to check on me. Sure glad you came instead. So how long are you stayin'?"

This is the part that twists my gut—leaving my kid brother behind, telling him my visit won't be as long as he'd like. "Just until I find Mama. You know that, Jace."

His shoulders slump.

"But I'm coming back next month," I add, thinking the reminder will lift his spirits.

"Yeah, but only for three days and you're gone again."

So much for that. Maybe I should tell him I'll come back the month after. Or that I'll stay longer next time. I decide to say neither because there's nothing I can tell him that won't be a lie.

Jace lets out a sigh, his cone almost forgotten.

Fuck. "How about you come out for one of the games?"

His eyes light up. "Can I stand on the sidelines with you and the team again?"

I shrug. "I don't see why not."

"Sometimes I can't believe you're my brother," he says, returning his attention to the melting cream. "And not only because you're this big famous quarterback, but because you're fun to be around, you know? Some of my friends—their brothers suck! But not you. You teach me a lot of neat stuff. About football… and girls." He grins and flips his new Redhorns hat to the back. "You're cool. Like me."

I lift a brow. "Don't you have that in reverse? It's you who's cool like *me*, kid."

"Yeah, that too." He chomps the bottom of his cone.

I lift my cup and take a pull from the straw, my attention moving toward the crowd of patrons assembled near the order window—pointing, staring, or pulling out their phones. It will only be a matter of minutes before the Blue Ridgers descend—demanding autographs, pictures, and conversation. None of which I'm in the mood for. Trying to preserve uninterrupted time with Jace, I steer him several feet out toward the sitting area. He straddles one of the benches and I mimic his position on the seat across from him.

He grimaces at the green juice in my cup. "Why are you drinking that?"

"Because it's healthier than that artificial crap you're eating." I extend the veggie drink to him. "Try it."

"Nah. I'm good with the artificial crap."

I chuckle.

"Hanging with you is the best even if it's only for ice

cream. Are you sure you can't stay an extra day?"

It's been less than twenty-four hours and coach is already losing his shit. Calling. Texting. Leaving messages. None to which I've responded. "I gotta head back, Jace. The playoffs, remember?"

"Yeah, I know." A flash of disappointment crosses his face. "I just wish we had more time together."

"I do, too, squirt." It's like he's programmed to say just the right words to kick me in the balls. *Every single time.* "But hey, we have today, so let's make the most of it, all right?"

He stuffs the last of the cone into his mouth and speaks around his food. "We have to find Mama first."

"No. *I* have to find Mama and you have practice. Let's get you back to the school. Jimmy and I will track down Mama, and we'll all be together by dinner."

"You think so?" he asks, his voice hopeful.

"Yeah. I'm sure she's fine," I say, as we pull away from the ice cream parlor.

Minutes later, I slow to a stop near the football field and Jace hops out of the car, throwing me a strange look before grabbing his bag.

My brows scrunch, wondering why he's staring with that wide grin of his. "Did I miss something?"

"Nope, I'm really glad you're home."

I frown, bothered by how easily he communicates his feelings. "What have I told you about emotions?"

"To push them down. But that's with other people, right? Not family. Not you and me."

"It applies to *everyone*," I say, my voice firm. "Emotions give way to weakness."

"But Mama says emotions are important."

I pinch the bridge of my nose. *Of course she does.* "Get going, Jace. You don't want to be late."

He reaches for his duffel bag, then looks back at me as if something has occurred to him. "I'll only do the emotions thing for Mama, okay? She likes it."

"It's fine, kid." I'll deprogram him later.

"You've shown emotions too, you know. Even today. I saw 'em. But you aren't weak, Branch. You're the strongest person I know." He leans in as if making sure no one hears. "Love you, big bro," he whispers, and then he closes the door, jogging off to join his teammates.

Dammit, Jace. That kid is determined to get under my skin.

I stare after him, remembering the days when I was stepping onto that same field. I flip off my cap, toss it on the seat, and run a hand through my hair, exhaling the worry I didn't want my brother to see.

Where the fuck is Mama?

Jimmy and I have no luck at the police station or the local hospitals. No one by the name of Mary McGuire is registered, and none of the Jane Does fit Mama's description. We drive around town for hours, checking spots she's mentioned or ventured off to in the past. But nothing.

Tired and frustrated, I fall quiet, racking my brain for any clue as to where she could be. And after perusing every lead, we still come up empty, but Denver promises to keep looking. This means more time in Georgia. I hate to deliver the news about Mama to Jace, but my spending an extra day in Blue Ridge will soften the blow.

Dinner at Jimmy and Loretta's is a reminder of the pages of a chapter that's best left untouched. The chapter some would entitle *Childhood*. Or *Good Luck, Hope You Make It*. Or whatever fucking term describes that time period. Was mine bad? That's still undecided. But if there was any good, it's directly attributed to Jimmy. Not to sell Mama short. I genuinely love Mary McGuire. Despite some of her stunts over the years, I know she's a loving mother. And I know she's a good woman. A good woman who's been served a raw deal. And aside from her condition, I'm convinced her biggest flaw is that she loves too hard.

My father, well, he was—and still is—one big shitload of disappointment, which is where Jimmy came in. After Dad left, Jimmy checked in on us as often as he could, sometimes every other day. Over time, those days became weeks, months, and years that Jimmy would pinch-hit for a man who didn't give two shits about what he'd left behind.

Jimmy became a man with two families, or maybe it was one big fucked-up family... I don't know. But Loretta—the saint she is—allowed him to have it. And even with the responsibility of being a wife and mother, she became a second pair of hands at the McGuire household, helping out on those days when Mama was unable to do much more than stare into space or carry on her one-sided conversations.

Loretta's help extended beyond the household chores of cooking, cleaning, and shopping. There were medical appointments, birthday parties, and gifts at Christmas. All the things a mother would take care of—she did. I knew then, as I do now, there's no way to repay that type of debt.

I glance between Loretta and Jimmy, the couple who give so freely of themselves but who've made a habit of refusing any gifts from me beyond game tickets. I decide on a new approach. Something they can't refuse as they have in the past.

Loretta is buried in conversation with Jace and her daughters about school and plans for the upcoming fall break, while Jimmy and I squabble over football stats and predictions for the playoffs. When Jimmy mentions my returning next month for the Blue Ridge Bowl, Jace's attention shifts, his eyes pinned on me.

"I'm still on the town council and we finally got started on the rec center I've been pushing for," Jimmy announces.

"Hey, that's great," I say and take a long swig of my beer.

"We had to pause construction, though. That tornado last spring did some real damage, so some funds had to be redirected."

"Sorry to hear that, Jim."

"We'll get it back on track. We expect tourism and donations to increase now that we've partnered with the local football star," he says and waggles his brows.

"Happy to help out."

"No, you aren't." He chuckles. "You hate coming back here."

True. But I don't say it aloud, and I wish Jimmy hadn't. Not in front of Jace. "I've already been roped into that annual weekend gig, so why not add an extra day? And it's cool the kids will have something here that I didn't."

"Yeah, and it's not like you'd miss the opportunity to be in the spotlight."

"Gotta keep my name on everyone's lips."

"No chance your name is forgotten anytime soon." He stares at me as we grab our plates and head to the kitchen.

"What's with the look?" I ask.

"It's good to have you here. Feels like the old days. Why don't you come by the garage tomorrow? Work on a few cars with me for old time's sake."

Now that I've seen for myself that Jace is okay, all my attention is reserved for finding Mama. "I didn't come here to work."

"I know. But imagine the prices I could charge if my customers know *the* Branch McGuire had his hands on their engines."

"That's not your style, Jim."

"Okay. It's not. But it would be a real treat for these people to know you worked on their cars. Come on. Just a few hours. You can hang out, sign a few autographs."

"What time do you want me there?" I figure work is a better alternative to climbing the walls or putting my fist through them, which is more than likely the reason Jimmy is making the effort to distract me.

"Let's say a little after one. You can close the place down with me and we'll grab a beer afterward."

"Are we leaving already?" Jace asks when he sees me heading for the door.

"Yeah. Long day tomorrow." I signal him to say his thank-you, and I follow his lead.

"Don't forget the keys to Crystal," Jimmy says.

"Already have 'em."

As a buffer to my Blue Ridge visits, Jimmy consistently hands over the keys to his mint-condition viper-red Corvette. He loves that car, and while he's fine with my driving it, he won't consider selling. I've *volunteered* to take it off his hands more times than I can count, even offering more than it's worth, but he says the car is a part of his family and he doesn't sell off family to the highest bidder.

He'd think differently if his family was like mine.

The next morning I receive a call from Denver. Someone who fits Mama's description is registered in the mental ward of a hospital two counties over. Thinking this could be another dead end, I decide not to tell Jace. No point in getting his hopes up.

After dropping him off at school, I pick up Jimmy and we head over to Union General. Jimmy Perez may wear the title of *close family friend*, but he's more of a parent. Always present for those times when a father should be. Not that I don't have a bio parent who holds that title, but Curtis McGuire is better suited for the role of distant uncle or cousin. He's been missing more than he's been around, except for football season, when he managed to show up without being asked.

I'd spot him in the stands—same seat every game. He never said a word to me, before the games or after. In fact, he typically left right before the games ended. I never understood why he bothered to come. At first, I figured it gave him a reason to boast—his son was the star quarterback. That's probably where it all started—my chasing the spotlight. Whenever I was there standing center stage, I had Dad's attention. And at times, it felt as if I needed the limelight more than I needed the sport I'd grown up loving. And now I'm so addicted to it I don't know how life would be without it. Was I still seeking attention from a man who wasn't worth the dirt he was made from?

Back then, I absolutely was. I played harder. I ran faster. I did everything I could to keep the focus on me. To keep *his* focus on me. Although angry, I wanted him there and I figured the better I played, the more likely he was to come back, and maybe, just maybe, he'd stay afterward. That never happened. And as suddenly as Dad started coming to my games, he stopped. I never understood why and I never asked.

After confirming Mama's identity, Jimmy and I walk down the hall to her room. I stand outside the door, bracing myself for any of the different Mary McGuires I'd encountered through the years.

"I can come in with you," Jimmy offers.

"Nah. I'm good."

He nods. "I'll go grab some coffee, then." He heads off in the opposite direction as I step into the room.

"Mama," I say, my voice low.

She looks up, her eyes narrowed, studying me as if I'm a stranger.

She battles heavy lids.

They win.

Her eyes close.

The nurse approaches, whispering when she's a few feet away. "Your mother's behavior was very erratic when they

45

brought her in. So she was heavily sedated. Now that we've gotten her records and treatment protocol, we're reintroducing her regular meds into her system."

I glance at the IV, my eyes following the line to Mama's arm.

"You may want to come back when she's a bit more normal."

Normal? Mary McGuire? I suppose there *were* times when she was normal. Maybe *normal* is an inaccurate label. But she was *her* version of normal. And that meant good times. The times Jace deserves.

"I'll stay until she's more herself."

Instead of taking that as her cue to leave, the nurse steps closer.

My brow rises. "Do you need something, sugar?"

Her tongue flicks across her lower lip, her gaze pinned to mine. "I have an hour break coming up. I can sit with you if you'd like."

I look her over. She's young, mid-twenties I'd guess. Cute face, decent-sized tits, tight little body. But I'm not here to fuck cute nurses with decent-sized tits. And that's all she'd get if I was. A long, hard fuck. There'd be no small talk, no questions about why she chose a profession in the medical field. Because I wouldn't care. For that entire hour, she'd have what she was asking for—my cock, balls deep inside her anxious little cunt. I'd get a release, maybe two. And then I'd send her on her way. "Not necessary, but thanks for the offer."

"No problem. And just so you know, I'm a really big fan. Really. Really. Big." Her eyes take a slow crawl over my body, assessing me from head to toe, her lips curving into a smile when her eyes finally touch mine. "Probably one of your biggest."

She's not yet discouraged. She should be. She's offered; I've declined. Any further advances only serve to degrade her and irritate me. I suppress the urge to tell her exactly that, but as I step past her, she adds, "Well, if you need anything or change your mind, here's my number." She jots it down on a piece of paper that she flips over, places to her lips, kisses on the back, then passes to me. "I'm Nurse Christina, by the way, and in case you're wondering, I don't have a problem *playing nurse* after hours." With a wink, she turns and exits the room.

My first instinct is to toss the scrap of paper, but something she said sparks an idea, so I tuck her number in my pocket and send Jimmy a text, updating him. No point in both of us hanging around.

I glance over the room and let out a sigh before stepping closer to Mama. I stare at her for a long stretch of time. She looks peaceful. Youthful, even. I press a kiss to her forehead and take a seat beside the bed, my hand resting on hers. Minutes stretch into hours before she shows signs of consciousness. Figuring she'll be hungry, I step out and make arrangements to have some decent food brought in.

Later, when I'm placing a tray on the bed table, Mama's eyes flicker to mine and there's a glimmer of recognition.

"Are you okay?"

She stares blankly.

"It's me. Branch."

"Do you think I don't recognize my own son? Come over here and give your mama a hug."

She looks like Mama, and except for the croaky voice, she

sounds like Mama. Still, I can't help but wonder which *version* of Mama is inviting me to step closer.

I push the bed table aside and lean down to her. She wraps her arms around my neck, and for the first time since hearing she was missing, air seems to finally move through my lungs.

I make sure she eats, noticing the color return to her cheeks with each bite. And I sit and talk with her for hours. I actually talk to *her*. Not to some bizarre rendition of Mary McGuire, but to the mama I try to hold in my memories, the mama I want for Jace.

And that's how I spend my afternoon.

Talking.

Reminiscing.

Laughing.

As if nothing's wrong.

As if she didn't scare the living fuck out of me.

As if she didn't leave my kid brother at home by himself for days.

I listen. And I can't help but smile at her while she goes on and on about one of the new neighbors and their horde of cats. Mama hates cats.

I even find myself laughing again. And if I hadn't seen the many sides of Mary McGuire, I'd swear she was fine.

But I know she isn't.

And I know she never will be.

Chapter
SEVEN

Branch

January 6, 2017

I WATCH MAMA WITH JACE. HIS FOREHEAD IS SMOOTH, his smile gentle. He seems more relaxed now that she's finally home. I wonder if this is the first time she's disappeared on him, or if it's simply the first time he's called me about it. I make a mental note to ask him later. Once he heads off to his room, I sit on the couch and broach the conversation that always ends badly.

"You can't go off your meds, Mama."

"I don't need those things. They mess up my insides," she says, a distinct quaver in her voice. "Have me feeling things that aren't real."

"That means it's time for a new cocktail of drugs. You can't go without them and you know that."

"I said, I don't need them," she repeats, her voice creeping higher.

"I'm not here to argue with you."

She peers at me with narrowed eyes. "Why *are* you here,

Branch? For your 'parade day'?"

I ignore her jab and deliver the threat that tightens my gut. "Either you stay on the meds, or I'm taking Jace back with me. It's your choice."

"No. No. No. You can't do that! You can't," she pleads, her expression frantic. "Jace is the only thing I have left, and we need each other."

"Then act like it. You have to be responsible. You can't leave an eleven-year-old kid at home for days by himself."

We pause our conversation when Jace enters the room, his happy appearance falling as he glances between the two of us.

"Why are you two always fighting?" he yells and turns to Mama. "You're the reason he won't come home more, aren't you?"

Her eyes flicker from me to Jace, an anxious expression crossing her face. She attempts to compose herself and reaches out to him, but he turns and rushes from the room.

"See what you've done," she says. "You drop in from your highfalutin life and turn my baby boy against me."

"Jace called *me*. What was I supposed to do? Should I have called Dad? You know he won't come within a hundred feet of you after what you pulled the last time he was here."

"That was not my fault, Branch. He had no business bringing his whore and her kid to our home."

"Not this again. You need to let all of that shit go, Mama."

"Branch Warren McGuire. Don't you dare speak to me like that!"

"Like what? It's the truth. Every time I'm here, it's the same story. 'Dad made promises.' 'Dad lied.' 'Dad cheated.' 'Dad needs to burn in hell.' I'm tired of hearing about what he's done or hasn't done. Talking about it isn't going to change anything. Don't you get that?" I hate to be curt with her, but she makes it next to impossible to be any other way.

She shakes her head in denial, her eyes filling with tears.

"Why not focus on something you *can* change? Like getting in with Dr. Blake, finding a new cocktail of drugs, and staying on track?"

"Even now. After all that man has done to us, you still side with him over me."

By now I've had enough. She hasn't acknowledged anything I've said. And once Dad's name is mentioned, everything else fades to black. And the same applies for me at this point. I tune it all out. Running a hand through my hair, I rest my head in my palms while she continues to berate the man I suspect she still loves. I've heard this story so many times I can recite it in my sleep. Mama wants to go on and on about shit that doesn't matter anymore. So I let her.

"Branch, do you hear me?" she asks when she finally notices my lack of response.

I half-heartedly lift my gaze to hers. The years I've tried to forget flash through my head, and I see my mother for who she is. I see eyes that match mine and I wonder if my anger will one day become the mental instability that sits in the shadows of hers. "I'm done with this, Mama. I'm gonna check on Jace."

Last night didn't get me anywhere, but today I won't accept Mama's backtracking. I hear her moving around in the kitchen and I join her.

"Good morning," she says when I sit at the table.

"Mornin', Mama."

"I'm sorry about last night," she says. "And to make up for it, I made these special for you." She sets a plate of strawberry-banana pancakes in front of me. This was the remedy as a kid. No way will I stuff this crap into my body now. She knows that. But to increase the likelihood of this discussion going down a little easier, I make a gesture and take a few bites.

"What happened? What's the real reason you stopped taking your medication?" I gulp a full glass of water to push down the shit I didn't want to swallow.

"I told you yesterday."

I watch as she moves around the kitchen, not convinced I know the whole story.

"I caught your game against the Patriots. Still my little star quarterback," she says, her eyes shining as she smiles at me. "You and that arm are gonna end up in the Hall of Fame one of these days. Mark my words."

She's almost as much of a football junkie as I am. Though it didn't start out that way. She hated my playing. Always afraid I'd get hurt like Dad. When she accepted I was going to play regardless of her fear, she came around. Now she's one of my biggest fans, and she knows I love talking football with her. But using this topic to divert the reason for my visit is not going to work.

I push the plate aside and lean forward, elbows to table. "I made an appointment with Dr. Blake for you."

Her smile fades. "Why?"

"I told you. You need to get back on track."

"Branch, I'm fine. Do I look like I'm sick in the head to you?"

"This is not up for debate. You're going," I tell her, my insides twisting when I see the hurt in her eyes.

"I'm the parent here." A tear slides down her cheek. "I'm the parent," she repeats, her finger jabbing her chest for emphasis. "I decide if I want to go to a damn head shrink."

"And I have custody of Jace."

I watch as everything she's holding up starts to crumble. I hate threatening her with that, but it's the only play I have when she gets like this.

More tears stream.

"Why do you hold that over my head? Would you actually take away the one thing I have left in this world? Do you resent me that much, Branch?"

"I only allowed him to stay because you were doing what you promised."

"*You* allowed him to stay? With his own mother? Who do you think you are, Branch? Jace is my son. *Mine.*"

"I didn't say he wasn't, but if you aren't doing what you should in order to be the type of mother he needs, then he can't stay here with you."

"Did Jace say something? Or is this all your doing? Maybe this is your way of getting back at me for something that's out of my—"

"Don't dare say this was not in your control because it damn well was," I say, the rage I've been nursing sweeping through my frame. "You left him alone for four fucking days, Mama!"

Shame shoots across her face and she turns away from me.

And I'm losing my patience with her, something I try to

avoid, but her obstinate behavior has ripped the last of my tolerance. "You *will* get the help you need, and if the threat of losing Jace is the only way to—"

"Fine. Fine. I'll go to your damn doctor." She slams her cup on the counter and storms out of the kitchen.

We drive the few miles to Dr. Blake's in silence. She's angry with me. I know that, and I deal with it, as I always have in the past. She puts up a similar fuss with the doctor, but once she realizes she has no choice, she gives in, tells him her latest symptoms, and he advises her on a new set of meds. We get the new prescriptions and head back to the house.

A half hour or so later, I pass the pills and a glass of water to her. "Dr. Blake says it takes anywhere from one to three weeks for these to take full effect, but they should at least start to kick in within the next forty-eight hours."

She reluctantly takes the pills from my hand. "Does that mean you won't let me out of your sight for the next two days?" she asks, her tone bitter.

"I hired a nurse."

"How convenient for you, Branch. I forgot how much of a hardship it is for you to be around your own mama," she spits out.

My jaw ticks and I let out a slow breath. "She's a friend of Jimmy and Loretta's. I've already met her. You have, too, but you may not remember. Her name is Christina. You'll like her."

She whips her eyes to mine. "Does it matter if I don't?"

I disregard her question and wait on her to swallow the pills, then check under her tongue when she's done. She's angrier now. And she will be for a while.

When the nurse finally arrives, I make the introductions. As expected, Mama is aloof, refusing to acknowledge Christina's presence. She crosses her arms over her chest, and after giving the perky, young nurse a once-over, she grimaces her disapproval and walks away.

I look down at Christina, not sure if Mama's reaction was due to the inappropriately tight and revealing nurse uniform, or to the idea of being monitored. Probably both. After giving our guest a tour of the house, I show her to her room, give some last-minute instructions, and head off to find Mama.

"I'm gonna head out, all right? I promised Jimmy I'd help out at the garage. I'll be back in time for dinner." I go to kiss her on the cheek, but she turns away from me. "Mama, you know I'm only looking out for you."

She pretends as if she's not listening, humming a tune I've come to recognize over the years. My eyes follow her as she grabs a bowl of fruit and heads out of the kitchen. She goes to the sewing room. I follow her, wanting to say something but not knowing what that something is. She pulls out her crochet needle and starts picking through a basket of yarn.

Her back is to me, but she knows I'm still watching her. "I'm proud of you, Mama," I finally say.

She starts to hum louder. And I know I'm wasting my efforts, so I give up.

Looks as if I'm in for another round of the silent treatment.

My sigh is heavy as I step away from her, exit the room, and walk out of the house. She said she was the parent, but why does it seem like all the responsibility rests on my shoulders?

Chapter
EIGHT

Ragan

May 5, 2008

"ARE YOU GONNA MAKE IT TO MY PARTY TONIGHT?" I'm in the school cafeteria with a group of friends chattering incessantly about the potential epicness of Hayley's birthday party. Her parents are out of town and trusted Hayley's Aunt Terri to serve as the official party patrol. But since Terri isn't much older than us, we'll have carte blanche to do whatever we want—hence the potential for epicness!

"Yep. I most definitely am!" I almost pinch myself to make sure I'm not dreaming. *I'm actually going to a party.* Eeek!

"A few kids from Dawson are dropping by, too," Hayley says, her pretty hazel eyes growing wide.

"Code for Ren Walker is dropping by," I tease.

"Fingers crossed. He's *really* cute and he said he'd bring a few friends."

"Code for hot jocks," Angela chimes in, munching on a

carrot stick and waggling her dark brows.

"So Ragan, you're honestly coming?" Hayley asks, unable to mask her surprise. "Cassidy is *actually* letting you out? I'm betting she'll change her mind at the last minute because she thinks you need to study."

I shrug. "Study what? We have only one more week of school, and my last final is next period."

"Yeah, but knowing her, she'll want you to know every word listed on our graduation program." Hayley laughs.

No one knows that my sanctioned getaways from *The House of Hell* only extend to school and work. So when asked why I never hang out, I lie and say it's because my parents are crazy strict about my studies. That's the only *reason* I figure they'll accept.

"That sounds like something she'd want but *so* not happening." I laugh, playing along with the lie. "I'm good to hang out tonight."

Patty won't mind at all. Of that, I'm 100 percent positive. My friends aren't aware of my living arrangements. Nor are they aware of my two lives—the one I spun for those outside of home and the real one. I've always been too afraid to let anyone—even Hayley—know about the real one. And even if I did have the notion to reveal the horrific details, there'd be consequences. Keeping quiet is my only choice.

"I can't believe we have to wait until June to graduate," Angela whines. "The building committee should've had a backup plan. Idiots."

"True. But hey, we'll be the first graduating class to walk across that stage," Faith adds.

"Yeah, we should do something crazy that will go down in history." Angela scans our expressions before revealing her suggestion. "Like mooning the audience."

Angela's ill-conceived idea is quickly dismissed and the conversation shifts back to the birthday bash. Angela, Faith, and Hayley chat in excited blurbs. About the party, the booze, the guys, and everything else a parent-free celebration could entail. Even with the bubble of excitement in my chest, I somehow mentally check out of the conversation, wondering how it would have been to have a healthy family like Hayley's. To look forward to celebrating my *born* day.

I'd never had a birthday party myself. The first time I asked Cassidy for one, she laughed, saying I was too horrible of a child and I didn't deserve a party. I took her words at face value, so the next year, I tried to prove her wrong. To do everything right and show her I was the exact opposite of horrible. But for all my efforts, I was still beaten on a routine basis and there was no party. According to Cassidy, I was a very bad girl and bad girls weren't allowed to have parties. Still determined, I asked for one the following year. And the next. Always receiving the same answer. I came to realize that no matter how well-behaved I was, I'd never have a birthday party.

And as unbelievable as it sounds, Hayley's will be the first one I've ever attended—outside of those for my stepsiblings. When I received any kind of party invites from friends in the past—and there had been several over the years—I was conveniently "studying" or "sick," and therefore unable to attend. That wasn't too far from the truth, considering the outcome—my impressive GPA, and thanks to a mother who used drugs the entire time she carried me, my immune system was shot to hell, so I was typically sick every other week anyway.

I awake in a strange bed, my brain foggy as to how I landed here, but I vaguely recall falling asleep next to someone. It must have been Hayley, but where is she? And why is the house so quiet? I rush to sit up and discover I'm completely naked.

Another detail that makes zero sense.

I stumble out of bed and search for my clothes. Panties under the pillow. Bra dangling from the lampshade. Shirt on the floor. Pants on the chair near the closet. *What the hell happened last night?* I dress in a rush—relieved that my cell is still in the back pocket of my jeans—and head out of the bedroom to find Hayley and some answers.

"Who are you?" I ask, shocked to find a tall, slender stranger in my friend's kitchen.

"Guess you overconsumed on quite a few things last night," he says with a silly-looking grin.

My brows scrunch. "What?"

He takes a sip of whatever is in his cup. I assume it's coffee.

"You seriously don't remember me?"

"Oh, forget it. It's too early in the morning for charades. Any coffee left?" I reach into the cupboard for a mug.

"No more K-Cups, but I made a fresh pot," he says and takes a seat at the kitchen table. He's still staring at me. A mocking smile traces his lips before he sips the coffee.

"Should I be sending out the stranger-danger call?"

He laughs. "Go ahead, but I doubt anyone answers. They

all went to IHOP. So it's just you and me, sexy."

No way would Hayley leave me here with this guy. "Yeah, right," I reply and grab the coffee pot.

He tilts his head, his eyes raking over me. "What? You don't think your girl would leave you here with me?"

"She wouldn't."

"She *did*. But I guess that's partially Ren's fault. He assured her I was harmless."

Well, that sounds about right. Hayley's mind turns to mush when a cute guy enters the picture. I grab the seat across from the stranger, take a long sip of coffee, and try to jog my memory.

"Now that you know it's only the two of us, are you still not interested in knowing my name? I mean, after all, I did fuck you last night."

The warm beverage spews from my mouth, some splashing his face while the rest appears as brown spots on his white T-shirt. "You did not," I snap at him.

He chuckles and lifts his shirt, using the edge to wipe the coffee from his face. "I even made you come. Twice."

Heat rushes to my cheeks.

"I guess I need to work on my pussy-eating skills." He flashes a wicked grin and leans forward, his elbows resting on the table. "Then maybe you won't forget next time."

My mouth falls open as my phone buzzes. A message from Hayley.

Good morning, Girl Gone Wild!

I send a reply text. *Call me now!!*

I focus on my cell, willing it to ring. And then I start to tick off the things that don't add up. This morning, I awoke naked, my clothes scattered about. I'd felt a tinge of soreness—down there—that I didn't understand, and now that I think about it, the sheets lingered with the slight scent of sex. I lift my gaze to the guy who I still insist upon labeling a stranger.

He winks at me, that silly grin still on his face. "Is it all coming back to you now?"

"I need to go. Talk to Hayley, I mean."

"That's a good idea. She can back up my story."

My brows scrunch. "How the hell would she know?"

"She walked into the room and saw my face between your legs. And by the way, your pussy..." He smacks his lips. "Mmm, mmm good."

"You're such a liar."

"You were naked when you woke up, right? How would I know something like that?" he asks.

"Maybe you're a Peeping Tom?"

"Okay, I'll give you that. But what about this? You have a tattoo of a butterfly at the top of your bikini line. Right below it is a smaller butterfly on a vine that spirals toward the tight little hole my tongue slipped into last night."

I stare at him, embarrassed that a stranger knows something so intimate, and angry that I have to try to recall the events of the previous evening.

"And there's a deep bruise on your upper thigh." His brows draw together. "What happened? Did you fall or something?"

"What *happened* is none of your business." That bruise is one of Cassidy's marks. A permanent reminder of where I came from.

After his question, there's no need to *try* to figure if there's any truth to his words. Because I know there is. No one, I mean *no one*, would know about that bruise unless they'd seen me naked. Which means I did have sex with him. And based on the way he's staring and teasing, he is planning on a *next time*. And we spend the entire morning talking about exactly that.

That day became the first of many I'd spend with Ethan Tyler. Within two weeks, he was my boyfriend and within a month, we were having sex on a regular basis. And not the sex I'd heard my high school girlfriends bragging about. I'm talking uninhabited sex—almost taboo—complete with role play, naughty outfits, butt plugs, and a slew of other toys. We didn't want to be apart and were soon making plans to get a place together. And nothing and no one would stop us.

"I really like him." I'm actually in love with him, but I don't tell Patty that.

"O-kaaay, but I sense there's more to this."

"Well, yeah. There is." I shift uncomfortably.

"So let's hear it."

"Ethan's asked me to move in with him. And I said yes," I blurt out in an excited rush.

"Wow. That's not quite what I expected. Why so fast, Ragan?" she asks, the concern apparent in her voice.

I shrug. "It doesn't feel fast to us. It just feels right."

Patty lets out a sigh and asks me to take a seat beside her. After a long conversation about the implications of growing up too fast, rites of passage, and living with a man, she suggests I take a couple of days to think about it. When I tell her I'm pretty sure my mind won't change in two days, she makes me promise to at least wait until after graduation. Since it's only two weeks away, I figure that's a good compromise. Plus it would take that much time for us to find a place anyway, so I agree to wait.

Ethan has a pretty decent job, so there are lots of dates, overnights at fancy hotels, day trips to amusement parks—to places I've always wanted to go. And we've done things I've always wanted to do. With my family. Like vacations and weekend getaways.

My friends always shared details about their summer breaks. I desperately wanted those same experiences. So I lied. I made up stories. Once I told them I spent the summer at the beach and that for fall break, my family and I went camping.

And when they went bigger with the truth, I went bigger with a lie, saying I'd gone to the Grand Canyon one summer break and to Disney World the next. No one was ever the wiser.

But Ethan turned all of those lies into truths. My life with him was as he'd promised. I was happier than I could ever remember being. No worries about using the wrong toilet paper or getting beaten for drinking the name-brand soda. There were no belts or slaps across the face. There was no wishing for a family I would never have.

Ethan's family *was* my family. His mom became my mom. And she insisted I call her that. When she learned I'd never had a birthday party, she surprised me with one the following year. They loved me and accepted me as one of their own. I finally had what I always wanted. *Happiness.* The pain of my past was behind me and I was looking forward to a bright future.

I had no idea what the next eight years of my life would entail, the joys it would bring, the love that would fill my heart, and the wounds it would heal. I also didn't expect the lows, the control… or the baby.

Ethan and I had a cute little one-bedroom apartment near the suburbs. For three years, we cut corners and saved like crazy for a down payment on our first home. We had several thousand dollars in the bank, excellent credit, and two cars. I was even considering signing up for some college courses to pursue a fine arts degree. Not too shabby for a girl, who a few years ago, was practically homeless.

But life with Ethan wasn't all rainbows and unicorns. Over the course of our relationship, he became increasingly distrustful and controlling. I often discredited it, putting a spin on it like most women in similar situations tend to do. I convinced myself that it was how he showed his love. But deep down, it often worried me.

There were other things, too. Like my circle of friends becoming smaller. All of those high school buddies disappeared and were replaced with Ethan's friends. There was suddenly no use for two cell phones, so mine was turned off, and we only used his. My social media account became *his* social media account. I could only spend money when he said it was okay. I only hung out with him or with someone he approved of. And even small things, like trips to the mall, required his permission. I went along with it. *All of it.* Never once objected. Ethan's dominance, and ultimately his control over my life, didn't happen all at once, so I didn't notice it at first. But when the shit started to hit the fan, I was overwhelmed by it.

Chapter
NINE

Branch

January 7, 2017

I STEP INTO THE GARAGE AND IT HITS ME—THE FAMILIAR whiff of dirty motor oil, the smell dredging up memories I'd buried several times over. Another reason to detest this town. Flashbacks taunt you at every corner.

Life back then wasn't as carefree as it should have been. Not much different from my current reality. But that's where distractions came in. *Football. Jimmy's Garage. Girls.* Those had been the predominant thoughts running through the head of a pubescent kid whose primary goal was relieving an ever-constant stiffy. I did some pretty wild shit in this garage.

"Hey, look who's slumming it today."

I grin at the greasy mechanic stepping from underneath the hood of a black Mustang. Matt Clark. The infamous whorehound who'd worked at the garage with me, and who's now Jimmy's right-hand man. Talk about wild shit. He was never too far from it either.

"I didn't know you were in town." Matt grabs my hand

and looks back at the others. "Look, fellas," he shouts over his shoulder. "Royalty has entered the building."

From the other side of the car come Chad and Todd, laughing as Matt makes a flimsy attempt to curtsy. I shake my head, cursing at the whole lot of 'em. We greet each other as if we'd hung out the night before, with wisecracks and bro hugs. It's nothing like the stars-in-the-eyes glances from fans, not even for a second. It's just four assholes cracking jokes and spewing garbage—the same group that was practically inseparable at Blue Ridge High.

"Didn't think we'd see you until next month for the charity bowl," Todd says.

I scrub a hand along my jaw. "That was the plan, but I had to deal with some family stuff."

They exchange glances, all knowing that's code for Mary McGuire drama.

"You know we can help out if you need us," Chad offers, his expression sympathetic.

"Nah. I wouldn't ask that of you. This is my responsibility."

"So, two hundred-fifty million, huh?" Matt asks, not-so-subtly changing the subject.

I nod. "Yeah, that sounds about right," I reply in reference to my new contract.

"Do you think you're *really* worth that?" Matt jokes.

I lean against the iron column next to the Mustang. "Dude, I'm worth a hell of a lot more than two hundred-fifty mill after that last game."

"Crazy how they tossed the Pro Bowl in the middle of playoffs this year, but that was a helluva game, bro," Chad pipes in. "I made over six grand on that one myself."

My brows shoot up. "You're still betting on me?"

"Every fucking time," he responds, a wide grin spreading across his face.

I shake my head at the balls on this guy. Last year, Chad and his wife were on pretty bad terms. He'd lost a shitload of money with fantasy league bets she knew nothing about. Nearly lost his house and damn near his marriage. Yet here he is, at it again.

I still fail to comprehend his inclination to marry Sherèe in the first place. Stupid move if you ask me. I shrug. *Better his problem than mine.* "Guess if you're gonna bet, you best do it on a sure thing."

"Still humble, eh?" Matt chuckles at his sarcasm and shakes his head.

"Hell, yeah. How would you recognize me otherwise?"

The one afternoon I'm dragged into feeds into the next couple of days that I spend working on cars, shooting the shit, and talking football. After a few cases of beer and the same stories we somehow bring up every year, I almost forget the reason I'm back in town. But when my phone rings and I see the name on the screen, the reason comes screeching back. It's the call I knew I'd receive sooner or later. The one that reminds me that I'm not in Blue Ridge to fuck off. I'm here to take care of a woman who won't—and sometimes *can't*—take care of herself.

I walk into a scene no child should ever witness—one that clenches my gut. Mama is pacing the living room floor, stripped down to her underwear and talking aloud as if carrying on a conversation with another person. My brother is sitting there on the couch, wide-eyed, watching it all play out.

A tornado of anger rips through me. "Jace, where's the damn nurse?"

"In the kitchen on…on…on the phone," he stutters. "She's calling Mama's doctor."

I pull the throw from the back of the chair. "You don't need to see this. Go to your room," I say, grabbing his arm and pulling him from the sofa.

He looks up at me, ready to oppose, but when he takes in my stern expression, he does as he's told.

I scramble to get Mama covered up, but when she becomes combative, claiming she's waiting on some dress options for her wedding, I know she's too far gone. I pull out my phone and dial 911.

"The combination of medications isn't working," Dr. Blake says.

No shit, Sherlock. "So now what?"

"We keep trying until we get the right cocktail."

Dissatisfied with his response, I furrow my brows. "In the meantime, we continue watching her go through episodes like this?" I observe Mama through the small panel of glass on the hospital room door. She's finally calmed down, no longer twitching or shouting. But her arms are still strapped to the sides of the bed, and she's staring at the ceiling, mumbling to herself. All I think is I'm glad Jace isn't here to see her like this.

I grab a seat as my phone buzzes. It's been every ten minutes. Like clockwork. I know who it is—either my press agent Connie or my sports agent Vaughn. They've been calling all fucking day. I'm expected at practice tomorrow, but I haven't checked in, and I don't plan to. There'll be consequences, but there's no way I can leave Blue Ridge right now. Not until I get Mama in a better place. And definitely not until I get Jace squared away.

I stay in the room with Mama, lying silently in a makeshift bed that barely tolerates the length of my frame. And I wait. As the medications work their way through Mama's system, I wait. And as visions of Jace watching our mom spiral out of control flash in my head and sicken my stomach, I wait.

The light of day swings into the shadows of night, my gaze pinned to the silhouette the big oak outside the window is casting on the wall. Its limbs play with the dusk of evening, projecting billowy images that appear as dark animated figures that have lost all sense of control... much like Mama.

I'm awake most of the night—as often as she is. She cries Dad's name and other unintelligible nonsense until nearly the crack of dawn. Not everything she says is gibberish though. Some of it is as plain as day. One day, in particular, is etched in both our heads—the day Mama brings up every time I'm home. The day Dad came over to the house with his new wife Charlene.

When Dr. Blake comes to check on Mama later in the morning, he confirms starting her on a new round of meds. And after his evaluation, I know for certain my trip has to be extended. That means no practice and no TV appearance. That means hanging around long enough to see if Mama's meds work.

Within a couple of days, the change in Mama is slight, but it's enough to where they've allowed her to move around the room at will. At times, she recognizes me, and at others, it's as if we're meeting for the first time. And then in the next moment, she's walking around mumbling to herself about her sister Gayle finding the perfect maid of honor dress for her wedding.

The following day, Mama finally shows signs of herself. And when she looks at me, I spot something familiar in the depths of her blue eyes. Something that lets me know she's on her way back.

Dr. Blake's confident he's gotten the right drug regimen and says if she remains stable for the next thirty-six hours, she can be released, but not to her own devices. After a few more recommendations from the psychiatrist, I step outside the room to process it all, unsure if I can. Or maybe it's that I don't want to. My eyes are pinned to the small window, still watching Mama, already sure of what my next step should be, but equally sure I don't want to take it.

"Hey," Jimmy says, stepping behind me. "'Bout ready to go check on Jace?"

"I suppose."

"How's Mary?"

"Doc tried a different set of meds and they seem to be the right mix. They'll monitor her for a while and then she'll be released. But he doesn't think she'll ever be in the shape she was before, so she can never be the sole parental figure for Jace."

"So what does that mean?" Jimmy asks.

"He wants someone to live with them… to kind of supervise Mama."

"In what way?"

"Administer her meds. Keep track of behavioral abnormalities."

Jimmy's brows draw together. "Supervise Mary? You?"

"Well, that's what he suggested." I shrug. "But you know that's impossible."

"So what are you gonna do?"

"I don't know. I guess I could check with a relative, but who's gonna want to uproot their life to come babysit Mama and Jace?"

"You know Loretta and I will do all we can to help."

"I wouldn't ask anything like that of you guys."

"Regardless, we're here. Whatever you need, let us know."

Fuck. I pace the length of the hall, continuing to curse under my breath. I suppose I could bring in around-the-clock staff, but Mama won't respond well to that. It needs to be family, but who? Doesn't take long for me to figure that one out—there's no one. So what choice do I have? "I hate this damn town. It always leaves a bad taste in my mouth."

"You're not talking about the town."

I hear the frown in his voice and halt my steps, looking up at him. "You know how it was, Jimmy. You know why I'm never in a hurry to come back here."

"Yeah, I do, but you shouldn't say that about your folks."

"Branch," comes a voice from behind us. We turn to see the shrink jotting notes on his tablet. "My nurse checked, and the longest your mother can remain in the hospital is seven days. For the most part, Mary's back to herself and she's not unmanageable to the degree of mandatory institutionalization. So she can be released to the custody of a relative or sent to a mental health facility. And I can tell you firsthand, most patients who truly aren't in need of in-patient care deteriorate pretty rapidly in that type of environment."

I let out a sigh.

Doc Blake extends a stack of pamphlets to me. "But here are a few brochures if you decide to go that route."

"But I don't want to leave Blue Ridge. All my friends are here," Jace says, his eyes darting from me to Jimmy.

"You're always saying you want more time with me. This way you'll have it," I say, knowing this won't be an easy sell. "You'll get a front seat to most of my games. Right there on the sidelines. How many kids get to do that?"

"But if I go with you, I won't have Mama and I won't have my friends. Why can't I have all three?" he asks, his eyes sad as he leaves the room.

"Jace," I call after him, but he doesn't break stride as he pushes out of the front door. "Jace!"

"Let the boy go, Branch," Jimmy says.

"He can't stay here. You know that."

"Looks like you have some decisions to make."

"What do you mean?"

"The kid feels like he's losing his mom. His dad is hit or miss. You're in and out of his life long enough to toss a football around with him for a day or two, and then you're gone.

He has no idea what stability looks like. Do you honestly want him to grow up that way?"

Before I reply, Loretta calls Jimmy to grab something from a shelf in the kitchen. I go to the front door and look out to see Jace sitting on the step, his head bowed as he looks down at his feet. It reminds me of a day when I was that young boy, sitting on the porch waiting on Dad. A day he never showed up. A day that faded into night.

I can't do the same thing to my brother. Jimmy's right. I can't leave Jace here and I can't force him from the only stability he knows. And then there's Mama. Who knows what condition she'll fall into without Jace?

Knowing the right thing and *doing* the right thing, well, that's a difficult choice. The part of me that knows I need to protect Jace is screaming at me to grab him as fast as I can and get him the fuck away from here. And the part of me that knows taking him is the wrong choice, fires a pang of guilt that furrows through my gut. To take him away from his home is cruel. To leave him behind is even crueler. It's misery. And he'll drown in it if he stays here with only Mama at his side.

My decision vacillates from one option to the other, neither compelling enough to force my hand. And then there's my professional obligation. It, too, is somehow left undecided. The Broncos game is tomorrow and I know it will be a next-to-impossible win if I don't play. That's one thing I can easily settle—I'm heading back to Dallas. I'll sort out the family dramatics afterward.

I draw up the plans in my head as I take the short trip back to the hospital. Jace will stay with Jimmy and Loretta for a couple of days. I'll play the game, take care of the shit I know I'll have to deal with from Coach and Vaughn, then it's back to Georgia to bring Mama home from the hospital. And then and only then, will I make the tougher decisions I need to make.

I cross the room as Mama looks up, a smile spreading across her lips. She's happy to see me. I know that's about to change.

"There's my boy," she says. "I was just talking to one of the nurses about you."

"Really? Which nurse?"

"It wasn't that Christina, if that's what you're thinking. Praise heavens. I don't like that one. And I don't like the way she puts herself on display for you. Her breasts hanging over the top of her uniform. And those tight pants. I don't see how she bends over, but somehow she manages to do it just fine when you're around. Don't think I didn't notice." She shakes a finger at me. "And don't think I didn't notice *you* noticing her. You were never one to keep your pants zipped, but for Christ's sake, don't whip out *Little Branch* for that one."

Relieved to see that she's *Mama,* I can't help but laugh at her. "So what did the nurse that you *do* like say about me?"

"She knows everything there is to know about your life in the NFL." She beams. "No surprise there. So I told her about your childhood shenanigans. They made her smile. Made me smile, too."

"Tell her I said thanks for taking such good care of my favorite girl."

"I will." She blushes and moves her hand over her hair, recovering the loose strands that play about her face. "Oh, can you autograph that for her?" she asks, pointing to the gray jersey on the bed table.

I grab the marker and pull off the cap. "What's her name?"

"It's Deidra. And she's just the sweetest thing. If you ever hire a nurse for me again, I want her. Not that trashy Christina."

I sign the jersey and turn back to Mama.

"I'm so proud of you, Branch."

"Thanks, Mama." I tuck the loose strands of hair she missed behind her ear. "How are you feeling?"

"More like myself every day."

"Good." I sit down beside her on the bed. "I'm about to head out of town for a game."

Her face falls. "You're leaving?"

"You knew I wasn't planning on staying for good."

"Just like your daddy, Branch," she says, flicking the switch in the bat of an eye. "You're gonna leave me to fend for myself."

"Mama, why do you say stuff like that?"

"Because it's the truth," she says and swats my hand away. "Aren't you the one always going on and on about how I need to accept the truth? Well, that's what I'm doing."

"No. What you're doing is the same thing you did to run Dad away." The words come out before I even realize it.

Her eyes widen. "Is that what you think? That *I'm* the reason your daddy left us and took up with that woman?"

"Mama—"

"Have you been talking to him, Branch? About me? I've told you for years to stay away from that man!"

With each word, her volume crawls louder and if I stay and try to make her see reason, it will only get worse, so I stand to leave, stepping away from her. "I can't do this with you. Jimmy is outside waiting."

"What about your brother? What about Jace? Are you gonna leave him behind with your *crazy* mama? Isn't that what Curtis said? That I was crazy? Did he tell you *he* made me this way?"

"Mama, you need to calm down," I say, my voice low, hoping to soothe her emotional outburst.

"Go. Just go." She waves me off. "Your brother and I will be just fine."

I look down at her. The tears streaming down her cheeks twist my gut into knots. I've got to get away from this. From her. "Bye, Mama."

I don't hug her this time. She won't accept it, and I don't feel like being that son who gives one simply to give it. Instead, I leave.

After providing additional contact information to the nurses, I head downstairs to Jimmy, who's waiting outside, and hop into his car.

He takes in my expression. "Are you gonna be all right?"

I shake my head on an exhale. "Just get me out of here."

Chapter
TEN

Ragan

July 4, 2016

I STAND IN FRONT OF THE FLOOR-LENGTH MIRROR IN THE silence of disbelief. They fit. *They honest-to-goodness fit.* The size-five denim shorts I grabbed by mistake from last year's Old Navy end-of-summer sale. After months of trying to conceal what pregnancy left behind, my figure has made its long-awaited reappearance. I never thought anything positive would result from a low immune system, but my recent illness pulled at my extra weight and ran off with it. It took a while for my appetite to return to normal, but when it did, I was so used to eating smaller portions that I kept at it. Little by little, more pounds disappeared.

"Hurry up, Ragan. They're cranking up the grill," Ethan yells from downstairs.

With a confident smile, I turn away from my reflection to start our holiday. The fourth of July with Ethan's family. Grilling, music, and the pool. "I'm coming. Let me grab CeeCee's bag."

A nervous buoyancy follows me down the stairs and into the living room. Ethan is scrolling through his phone when he looks up and sees me in the doorway. Butterflies move over my stomach as I await his reaction to the *new me*, but my heart sinks when I see the scowl forming on his face.

"You're not wearing those," he says matter-of-factly, his gaze pinned to my shorts. "You need to change."

I look down at the recycled denim. "Why? I thought you'd like this." I pirouette with a smile. "See. I've lost weight."

"Turn around again," he says. "And bend over."

Although confused, I do as he asks.

"That's why. Those are too fucking short and you know it. Go change."

Is he kidding me? He doesn't acknowledge my weight loss, and he says nothing about my appearance. I'm also wearing lip gloss and eyeliner. And I *never* wear makeup. "I happen to like the way these look and I'm wearing them."

He looks up from his phone again, obviously surprised by my refusal.

"And I said, you're not."

"I'm not going to let you dress me, Ethan."

"If you think I'm letting you walk out of this house look-ing like that, you've lost your fucking mind."

"Why are you being so freaking mean? And looking like what? It's summer. These are shorts. I'm not changing."

He shoves his phone into his pocket. "You sure as fuck will change," he yells. His six-foot-two-inch frame reaches me in three long strides and he pushes me toward the stairs.

"Stop it." My tone is low, not wanting our daughter to hear us.

"What the fuck are you trying to prove? Get your ass

upstairs and put on some decent clothes so we can go."

His fingers are at my waist pinching and twisting my skin as he forces me to our bedroom. The years of abuse I've fought like hell to bury suddenly resurface and I'm terrified. And for a moment, I revert to the child who was unable to defend herself—trembling, vulnerable, and confused. "You're hurting me. Stop it, Ethan."

"You've lost a little weight. Now you think you're gonna show your ass to anyone who wants to see?" He rubs his fingers roughly over my mouth, smearing my lip gloss. "So you think you're beautiful now?"

"What's wrong with you? Why are you doing this?" I move to get away from him, but he holds me in place while aggressively pulling at my shorts.

"Ethan, stop it," I scream. "Get away from me."

"I'll get away from you when I'm good and damn ready," he snarls, slamming my body into the bedroom wall and landing a solid blow to my stomach.

Air rushes from my lungs and I keel over, my forearm cradling my abdomen. Not allowing me the chance to recover, Ethan's arm curls around my midsection, lifting me and hurling me onto the bed, his frame covering mine.

I gather all my strength and try pushing him away. "Fucking stop!"

But he doesn't. He slaps me hard across the face and fists my hair, his other hand at my throat.

"Your body is for my eyes only, and you fucking know it!"

His grip on my throat tightens, cutting my breath. My legs rustle beneath him. "Please don't do this." Tears flood my eyes, thick and heavy, spilling down my cheeks in endless streams. "You promised you'd never do this. You promised!"

His weight presses into my thighs and I can't move. I'm no match for his strength, yet I manage to free my hand and drive a fist into his chest. He returns my blow with several of his own. My first instinct is to curl into a ball and take the abuse, same as I did when I was a kid, but then I hear Cecelia cry out. And that's what saves me. The cries of our daughter stop her father from beating me to a bloody pulp.

Ethan's fist is midair as he turns away and catches sight of CeeCee. Alarmed that he's been caught, he jumps off me and rushes from the room.

I sit up a little too fast, lose my balance, and fall from the bed. Cecelia is still standing in the doorway, tears streaking her cheeks. I gather myself from the floor, wiping away the blood that I know is scaring my daughter. I pull her into my arms and rock her back and forth to quiet her screams. To take away her fear. To remove the image of her mommy and daddy fighting. I rock and rock. And silently, I weep, holding my baby girl against my chest, afraid to move from this spot, and knowing I've reached the end of my story with the man I foolishly believed was my knight in shining armor.

Chapter

ELEVEN

Branch

January 14, 2017

FUCK.

Another sack and the quarter has barely started.

Get your head in the game, McGuire.

It's still raining. Doesn't appear it will let up anytime soon, either. But that's not the problem. I've played in rain before. The problem is the person the Redhorns are relying on. The problem is me.

The team is an array of confusion and frustration. The coach is spitting expletives up and down the sidelines, and the stands are a mass of expectant red and gray ponchos. And me, well something inexplicably fucked is going on. Something that never happens to a player of my caliber. Something I can't seem to shake.

Just as quickly as the players break formation, they are covered in a sea of midnight green and black—the Eagles defense isn't giving an inch. I take a few steps back looking for Tucker. He breaks free and I send the ball sailing toward him. A throw

I typically make with my eyes closed lands on the sidelines.

Shit.

The disappointment of the crowd echoes across the field, but I manage to tune it the fuck out and step out of the huddle for the next call.

Fourth down.

With less yardage and more pressure to make a play, an unfamiliar tension tightens around my eyes. If I don't get my shit together, no way will we make it through this round.

I line up on the center and call the play. Bosa snaps the ball. Dropping back, I look left, pump fake, and roll to my right. I tuck the ball and run through the line, shove a defender, and look down the field. Tucker is wide open. I lift the ball and prepare for the throw, but my eyes glaze over and a vision of Jace clouds my view. He's staring up at me… wanting, needing, expecting. I blink, attempting to regain my focus, but it doesn't come. This time, Jace is sitting slumped over Jimmy's steps, waiting, confused, desolate. I push the images back, clearing my head, and prepare to release the ball. I cock back and wham.

I'm down again.

And not by one or two players—it's more than what's necessary. Typically the opposition never has a chance to even grasp the tail of my jersey, let alone take me down, but they've spotted an opening tonight and they're seizing every opportunity to eliminate the greatest threat.

"Watch it, Anderson," I warn the Eagles defender.

"What's the problem, McGuire?" he sneers. "Can't stand the heat? Thought you were *The Man on Fire*."

I make a play for him, but Tucker grabs me, pulling me back.

Anderson smirks and walks off, his teammates guffawing and slapping him across the back.

End of the third quarter.

I look at the clock as I make my way to the sidelines. Down by two touchdowns.

"You all right, Branch?" the water boy asks, lifting the bottle to my lips and squeezing the liquid into my mouth. I spit it out and pace the line, the coach in my face demanding answers.

After the first few words of his would-be reprimand, I tell him to fuck off or sideline me. And I fucking mean it, I won't take his reproach on top of everything else.

The players throw me looks. Some curious. Some angry. But my don't-even-fucking-try-me scowl easily redirects their attention.

In less time than I'd like, we return to the field. My focus remains diverted throughout the better part of the game, but somehow toward the end, I manage to pull my head out of my ass long enough to barely get the win. *By two fucking points.*

In the span of seconds, my teammates shift from what-the-fuck-is-going-on to celebrating, popping and spraying bottles of Cristal, and giving me congratulatory slaps on the back. Something for the first time I know is unwarranted.

True to form, newscasters push their way through the crowd, hoping for the first response from *The Man on Fire.*

Microphones are shoved in my face. Cameras flash. Questions asked.

"Branch, was the strategy to give the Eagles a false sense of hope so they could lower their defense?"

I cast my eyes forward, my response stuck in the back of my throat.

"Was Coach Fobbs bothered by what appeared to be a total disregard for his plans tonight?" asks a different reporter.

Then comes question after question, the press firing them off in rapid succession. I push past them all and head to the lockers, something I've never done without my time in the limelight. Vaughn won't like it and I know he'll be right behind me. And before I finish the thought, he's hot on my tail.

"What the hell was that, Branch?" he demands, already pacing the floor.

"It was a *win*. We made it through another round of the playoffs, V," I flare off. "Or did you miss that?"

His brows draw together, sizing me up. "Come on. We're not going to play this game, are we? You know it's never just about the win for you. It's about showcasing your talent. But you haven't been the same since you went off the grid last week. Anything I should know?"

"Like what?" I'm not in the frame of mind for this bullshit and if he doesn't drop the inquisition, he's going to see a side of me he doesn't know exists.

"Did something happen in Georgia? Has one of those girls finally fucked with your head?"

I grimace. "Hell no. You know that will never fucking happen."

"Then what is it?" he asks, not letting up on his interrogation.

"It's nothing. Just a little off. It happens."

"Not to you."

I toss my helmet to the floor. "Drop it, Vaughn. This isn't the time." But he's right. Even on my worst day, it never happens to me. I'm never *off*.

"Look, you're in a position to up that two-hundred-fifty million. And I'm working my ass off for those two new endorsements we discussed last week. *Branch McGuire… The Man on Fire*. That's what they're lining up for. If there's even the slightest chance you can't perform at the top of your—"

"I got it. I'm good. Your three percent is safe, all right?"

He squints, tilting his head. "Now I *know* something's up. We've never gone there. In all the years I've represented you."

"It's family shit. Stuff I need to deal with," I finally spit out.

Understanding and sympathy cross his features. "Your mother again?"

I drop to the bench, leaning forward, my elbows propped on my knees. "Yeah."

"I see. It's never affected you like this on the field before though."

"I know."

"What's different? Has she regressed?"

"She's never been like this. I mean, she's been doing wild shit for as long as I can remember, but she was somewhat stable. But now, it's… I've not seen her like this in years. And my kid brother…"

"Jace? Is he okay?" Relaxing his stance, Vaughn joins me on the bench.

"I thought so. Not so sure anymore. And today… every time I looked down the field, I saw him. Looking up at me. Expecting me to—hell, I don't know. Fix some shit that can't ever be fixed."

Vaughn is quiet. Processing. Thinking. And then he finally asks, "Think you need to spend some time with Doc Pattington?"

"The team shrink? Nah." *Why the hell is he suggesting that?*

"Then what are you planning to do? Obviously this is something you need to take care of."

Noise rumbles through the locker room as the players grow closer. I toss Vaughn a look, signaling he should table this discussion.

"I get the feeling this won't be one of your party nights."

I shake my head. "Nah."

"Didn't think so. I'll meet you at your place within the hour."

"Hey, McGuire. Is your agent giving you plays now so you can up your price?" Tucker throws out with a chuckle.

"Fuck off, Lance."

"Dude, I'm not knocking you. It was risky. But good thing you knew I was a sure thing, baby."

"Is that what you call it? The only sure thing on this team is yours truly."

"One hour, Branch." And with that, Vaughn takes his leave from the impending hysteria.

Vaughn paces alongside the wall of windows that serve as my barrier to the outside world. I sit back in the large leather chair—bare-chested, bare feet, gym shorts, and beer in hand—watching as he goes back and forth, scrubbing a hand across his jaw, running his fingers through his hair, and occasionally mumbling to himself. He finally turns to meet my eyes. "As I see it, playing you and upsetting the status quo isn't the way we want to handle this. If everything works in our favor, we'll have five games left. I'm going to be honest here. I don't think you should play."

My grip tightens around the bottle. "What the fuck?"

"Hear me out," he says and takes a seat across from me. "You've been playing for years, Branch, and never has anyone questioned your performance. Never have you faltered. It'd be entirely different if this was something that happened from time to time. But it has *never* happened. That leads me to believe you can't put your personal life aside for the professional at this point."

"Vaughn, no one is fucking perfect."

"But that's what you've shown the league. Over and over again. Are you honestly fine with tonight? With the distinct possibility it can happen again?"

I take a long swig of my beer. "It won't."

"I'm honestly fine either way. But this is not the Branch McGuire you've asked me to sell. This is not the Branch McGuire you've wanted me to accept, so why would you?"

"You don't get it, do you? I have some serious shit going on."

"I realize that and I respect that. So take some time and take care of it. What if you sit out the rest of the season, give you some time to get your house in order, so to speak. That way, we won't risk your standing. Your stats are good, Branch. Too fucking good. They're unheard of. But your completion percentage dropped tonight. Too many more games like this one and it's all over."

"Are you not hearing me? I said I won't let that happen."

"After tonight, can you guarantee me that?"

"Come on, Vaughn. No one but me could have brought a game like that to victory."

"You get no arguments from me there. What you did was nothing short of miraculous, and the comeback may have even tipped the scales in your favor, but you and I both know you were off your game. And I'm betting we weren't the only ones who noticed."

"Percy?" I ask, referring to the team owner.

"Yes."

I've never sat out. Not once in all the years I've played. Playing is to me what therapy is for Mama. It cures what ails me. It makes me invincible. And it clears my mind of all the garbage that riddled my youth. Playing has become a necessary outlet. It's my fuel. And I don't know how I'll cope without it.

"I'm sure you noticed… and felt the impact," he says, his eyes darting to the bruise on my shoulder. "But the lack of focus placed a target on your back. What if you'd been hurt? A player with an injury on record loses marketability. Better you bow out for a while, regain focus so you're at the top of your game when you return."

The validity of Vaughn's argument pushes me to reconsider. "Let me think about it."

"While you're mulling it over, think about this. There's another endorsement on the table. One I haven't mentioned."

I lean forward, curious as to why he's kept this to himself and anxious to know the reason for the Cheshire cat smile. "Who is it?"

"Raine Industries."

My brows furrow as I try to place the name.

"You've heard of multibillionaire Aiden Raine, right? Well, his company has their hands in a little bit of everything. And I mean *everything*. I've done the research, and whatever they touch turns to gold. Make that *platinum*. Well, they've recently acquired the top footwear, sports, and casual apparel manufacturer in the country, and they're doing a massive overhaul. New branding, spokesperson, the whole gamut. And they want the best. Which means you. They want *you* in front of this."

"Are you shitting me?"

Vaughn's brow arches. "Do I ever kid around about your money?"

"Fucking hell. This could be huge."

"This *will* be huge. So huge in fact that Raine's not sending his people. *He's* coming himself. That's how big this is. He and his wife are headed out of the country and want to drop in for a face-to-face. We'll have lawyers on standby to finalize the details if all goes according to plan. Any exposure for you in this capacity is money in the bank for Percy. If we get this signed, sealed, and delivered before the next playoff game, it will go a long way to coax him over to our side."

I nod, my anticipation already growing. "And I highly doubt he'll say no when such a heavy hitter is in the picture."

"Exactly." Vaughn stands to leave. "Twenty-four hours. That's all we've got to get in front of this. So think it over, and if you agree with my approach, I'll come up with a way to sell this to Percy. If they make it past the playoffs without you, you're going to have to play the Super Bowl. No way will he be on board with you skipping that unless you're dead.

Besides, that's your winning ticket. We need you in that one. But I'm pretty sure that with the right spin, we can sideline you for the other four. Maybe get you to commentate or do some spotlights. I'll figure out something." His gaze falls to my arm again. "And ice that shoulder."

The familiar ding of an ESPN alert has me moving toward my phone. *Branch McGuire. How long will he remain The Man on Fire?* I scan the article and a stream of obscenities crosses my lips. I'm not accustomed to derogatory statements paired alongside my name. I close the app and press the speed dial for Vaughn.

That one article alone is enough to force my decision. Last night could have very easily gone the other way. Luck may have been on my side, but I preferred my skill to any fucking luck. Like Vaughn said, more games like last night and it's all over. Not my football career, but my ranking. And I won't risk something I've busted my ass to achieve. I finish the call with Vaughn, deciding to meet over lunch to discuss a game plan.

The next day, I'm on a plane headed back to Blue Ridge, my spirits low as I get in the headspace to deal with Mama. As the plane makes its ascent, I decide it's also time to face Curtis McGuire. Jace doesn't want to leave Blue Ridge and I sure as hell don't want to make it my home again. So it's time to determine if the man I'd held out hope for is ready to be the father to my brother that he wasn't to me.

Chapter
TWELVE

Ragan

January 3, 2017

AFTER SIX MONTHS OF LIVING WITH HAYLEY AND her parents and with zero financial support from Ethan, my pride gets the better of me. I can't continue to live as a freeloader despite their insistence to the contrary. My bank account has dwindled to nothing, leaving me unable to pay for personal expenses, let alone chip in for my part of the food. And to make matters worse, last Friday was my last day working for Dr. Koscner.

The problem with being the product of a crack addict— well, one of the many problems—is a high susceptibility to illness, a trait I passed along to my baby girl Cecelia. So through a cycle of my being out sick from my job or CeeCee being home sick from day care, I've missed work more than my employer can accommodate, which leaves me jobless and almost penniless.

Circumstances may have left me short on pride, but since there is still *some* left, I take it and my baby girl and leave the

Millers. If anyone owes me anything in this world, it's Dad. So that's where I end up. On his doorstep. Literally down to my last dime, I find myself standing in front of a door that once camouflaged the hurt and dysfunction of those who should have been a family but never were. I lift an unsteady finger to the doorbell, and my belly clenches as I fight back the sudden wave of nausea.

Over the past eight years, my relationship with Dad has been nonexistent. And Ethan would become incensed at the mere mention of Dad or his attempts to reach out, claiming he wasn't a father when I needed one, so to hell with him now. The part of me that went along with everything Ethan wanted agreed without question. But the part of me that wanted some type of connection with the man whose blood runs through my veins disagreed. Yet I never voiced it aloud. I kept quiet and pretended we were of the same accord. And in doing so, I think I even convinced myself that I was in complete agreement about Dad. I mean, he'd never been a father to me in any sense of the word, so why pretend to be something we weren't? And to be frank, I felt stupid for wanting anything to do with a man who leveraged my childhood, my safety, and my overall well-being as a means to satisfy his own selfishness.

I squeeze CeeCee's little hand, and on a shaky exhale, I push the button. Two deep breaths later, David Prescott opens the door.

I didn't bother calling. CeeCee and I just showed up, bags in hand. So the surprised expression that marks Dad's features is expected. Ignoring his shock, I don't mince words. I get to the point, telling him we need a place to stay until I get on my feet. I know he and his she-devil of a wife have divorced; otherwise, I would have swallowed *all* of my pride and stayed a little longer at Hayley's.

While Dad registers *his* disbelief, I take a moment to survey him. He looks the same but different. As if he's aged twenty years instead of eight. He still has a full head of hair—straggly, salt and pepper, and long overdue for a haircut. A shave would do him some good, too. His brown eyes are sad, but light up as they fall on my daughter. And when he looks back to me, an unexpected smile spreads over his lips.

He invites us in, and amid the further bouts of shock and unfamiliarity, he appears genuinely happy to see us. Maybe because he has no one else. Maybe because he views this as an opportunity to fix what he allowed to break. Or maybe it's because of CeeCee.

And then there's my reaction to him. My heart squeezes a margin, enough to stir emotions I can't quite put a finger on. Maybe, just maybe, a pea-sized part of my being, a part buried deep, deep inside of me is happy to see him, too. But I shouldn't be. I should hate this man as much as I hate Cassidy. I know it. And I suspect he knows it, too.

This is Dad's first encounter with his granddaughter, so he takes some time with her. Asking her name, making her laugh, and getting better acquainted.

Awhile later, he shows us to my former bedroom. I take in the small space that has barely changed over the years. And as my eyes scan the room, the memories of my first whipping from Cassidy suddenly flood my thoughts.

"Go to your room," she orders.
"Why? What did I do?"
"Don't talk back."
"I just want to know what—"

She points a finger at me. "I will not say it again."

I look toward Dad.

"Listen to your mother, Ragan," he says.

"She's not my mother," I yell.

"Ragan, go to your room," he repeats, impatience filling his tone.

I storm off down the hall, slamming the bedroom door once I'm inside. Moments later, the door swings open and in steps Cassidy.

"I will not put up with your disrespect. Do you understand?"

"I do the same as your kids, but they never get in trouble," I try to explain, not understanding the difference between my behavior and that of my stepsiblings.

"They do not talk back. They do not yell and slam doors. They do not break things and lie about it. It's you. It's always you. But that stops today." She closes the door, grabs one of the belts hanging from a hook on the wall, and moves toward me.

The malevolence of her expression pushes me farther into the room. She meets me, step for step, until I'm nudged between her and the bed.

"I'm sorry. I won't be bad anymore," I whisper as a tear slides down my cheek.

Ignoring my apology, she shoves me onto the bed. I scramble to get away from her, but how can a seven-year-old overthrow the strength of a violence-induced adult?

She pulls at my pants, tugging them down until my bottom is exposed and then the belt meets my skin.

Still scrambling to get away, a loud shrill sound escapes my throat.

She pins me down, trapping me beneath her.

Another tear across my skin.

I scream for Dad, but he doesn't come. My yelps increase in volume, so she pushes my head into the mattress, muting my cries as slash after slash of the belt meets my backside, the bites like nails into my flesh. She continues until all my fight is gone. Until my body is limp. Until she is out of breath. And then finally, she stops, drops the belt on the floor, and walks out.

The next day I awaken in bed. It's bloodstained. I'm sore. I'm embarrassed. I don't understand what I did wrong, and I start to cry again.

I'd been in my room all night. Had gone to bed without dinner. No one seemed to care. And no one checked on me.

As I sit up, the door opens and Cassidy steps inside. I'm frightened. Too frightened to move. Too frightened to speak. She doesn't say anything either.

She strolls across the room to the bed, assesses my bruises and realizes damage control is in order. "You know, I was thinking, with a little makeup, you'll look like a little princess. Get cleaned up and I'll be right back."

She sounded weird. Nice. And she is never nice. At least not to me.

When she returns, I'm dressed and standing in front of the mirror. Staring at the dark bruise around my eye, Cassidy sits me down and makes a game of applying makeup to hide the marks on my face. She even gives me tips on how to reapply concealer if I happen to rub it off by mistake. I'm seven years old and I'm wearing makeup. Not to make me look like a princess, but to cover the bad she's whipped into me.

Nothing was the same after that. I was always on high alert. Always waiting for the next beating and flinching every time she approached me. I even find myself doing it now when someone gets too close.

I shake off that memory, but more follow. Recalling every corner I'd run to. Every position Cassidy forced me into. Flashes of the many times I lay naked across that bed as she beat the shit out of me. It all crashes into my mind. My stomach churns, and I take deep breaths to hold back the vomit. But I can't turn my mind off. It retrieves the onslaught of the pain, the hurt, and the fear. It stabs my insides like a knife, ripping me apart.

I stand frozen in place and think over the shattered beginnings of my life. I was born to a drug addict mother who abandoned me at age four. I was left with a dad who saddled up with the most horrible woman to have ever walked the planet. I was abused since the age of seven and terrified into keeping secrets. I was convinced Cassidy would kill me or send me someplace far worse if I ever told. So I grew up with no sense of feeling protected from my parents. And this is where it all happened. In this house. In *this* room.

I tell Dad I can't stay in a space that was nothing less than a childhood torture chamber. CeeCee and I take Noah's former room instead. Although it holds sad memories as well, they're more tolerable. I sit on the edge of the bed and wonder where Noah is. How he's doing. If he's finally happy.

After being forced from my home, I had no way to check on Noah other than going to his school. But when Cassidy found out, she intervened and warned me to stay away if I wanted to keep him safe. Noah was three years my junior, but he was small for his age—very frail and timid. So hoping to protect him, I did as she said. I stayed away.

After a few months of no contact with Noah, I received a Facebook message declaring he was running away. I hurriedly sent a reply, but I was too late. The account had been deactivated. Half out of my mind, I went to the school demanding answers, but they knew nothing. I even stormed into Dad's house and he was as clueless and unconcerned as always. He made no attempt to even look for his son, saying that if Noah didn't appreciate the roof he placed over his head, he was welcome to stay elsewhere. I went to the police, filed a report, but there were never any leads. They even questioned Cassidy and Dad, who both, of course, left out any mention of the truth behind Noah's disappearance.

A year or so later, I received another message from Noah, letting me know he was safe and not to worry. That he'd met a nice family that had taken him in. And that's where he planned to stay. Far away from the hurt and damage of the past. And I understood the need to do that... I only wish he hadn't run from me as well.

Once CeeCee and I are settled, Dad says we can stay as long as we need, and he gives me cash for food, gas, and personal items. He also tells me something that reaffirms my stay will be no longer than what's absolutely necessary.

His sister Sophie and her husband Stan are living with him temporarily as well until their new home construction is complete. Stan made a pretty good living driving for an Iowa-based trucking company, and when they relocated to Blue Ridge, so did he. He even helped get Dad's foot in the door at J&S Trucking, and soon after, he was offered a job. That meant he would eventually be going on the road with my uncle, which would leave me at home with my judgmental harpy of an aunt. She claims to be a woman of faith, but whatever she's selling, I ain't buying.

After dinner, Dad mentions a diner that's hiring. He

knows the owner and can put in a good word for me. Although he doesn't suspect the pay is great, he says if I make nice and smile real pretty, the tips alone should bring in decent earnings.

Make nice? Smile real pretty? Fat chance of that shit happening. I can barely manage a decent conversation with folks nowadays. Piling on the extras requires a bout of energy I can't afford to extend.

I later learn Aunt Sophie is on the church's prayer team with some woman by the name of Jolene. She's married to the owner of the diner. So Dad's pretty sure that between him and my aunt, the job is mine if I want it. Not that I have aspirations of waiting tables, but it's better than having repeated handouts from a man I'm not quite sure I can consider a father. Not only that, I need to save up enough money for a lawyer to get Ethan in court. He swore if we ever broke up, he would do right by CeeCee. But like everything else with Ethan Tyler, it was a lie.

Naïve. That's one word to sum up the person I was when I met Ethan. But never again. Never again will I fall for smooth lines and pipe dreams. And never again will I look for happy endings and rainbows. Why would I expect those given how my life started? I figure it will end much the same as it began—hard and hopeless. Happy endings and knights in shining armor. Bullshit like that simply isn't meant for a girl like me.

In the span of six months, all the baby weight I'd lost is back plus a few extra pounds for good measure. That's what depression can do for ya, I guess. I stare at my reflection in the mirror, wishing I were that size five again. To actually wear the outfits I want, instead of those that hide what I don't want to see.

I let out a sigh and head to the kitchen for breakfast. I'm hoping Aunt Sophie has left for her church group, but no such luck—she's still in the kitchen when I sit at the table.

"Are you sure you should eat that?" she asks, watching me pile food onto my plate.

I look up at her judgmental grimace. "If you didn't want me to eat it, then why did you cook it?"

"For your uncle and your father. I always prepare this for Stan when he leaves for long trips. It's sort of our tradition. And since David is heading out on the road with him, I figured he'd enjoy it, too," she says and removes the plate of flapjacks and bacon. "I prepared this for you."

I look down at the banana, strawberries, and whole wheat toast.

"Less calories," she says and tosses the pancakes and bacon into the trash.

I push back from the table. "I'll grab something at work."

"Suit yourself, Ragan. I'm only trying to help. You need a husband and Cecelia needs a father. You won't find either looking like that."

"You know, Aunt Sophie, you haven't changed a bit."

She gives me the once-over and frowns. "Neither have you."

I hate to leave CeeCee with my wretch of an aunt, but she adores my daughter, and although it took a while for it to happen, CeeCee seems to like her, too. I give my baby girl a goodbye kiss and head out the door.

I settle into my 2008 Jeep Liberty, pull on my seatbelt, and start the ignition. My phone beeps and I look to see a text from Ethan. It's the same lie he's been repeating for months. *He's sorry and wants to start over.* I delete the message and toss the phone into my bag.

And then, instead of backing out of the driveway, I sit and stare through the windshield, my hands gripping the steering wheel as I study the red brick house with its outdated white shutters. The house I grew up in. The house that scarred my mind and my body. And without notice, I start to cry.

I can't believe this is my life. *I just can't.* That's when I realize how much I hate the existence that is Ragan Prescott. I hate what it's become. I hate it all… my appearance, my finances, my joke of a family, my endless suffering. Even getting out of bed each morning has become an unnecessary encumbrance. Death has to be easier.

But I fight the urge to take the easy way out. I have to… for her, for my sweet baby Cecelia. If she were not my sole reason to keep breathing, I wouldn't. I'd make certain my second attempt at suicide was successful.

The first time I tried to leave this world behind, it was because of Cassidy. I was twelve years old, and all I could think of was getting out. Getting away from that sadistic monster. Not hurting anymore. Not being beaten down anymore.

I'd locked the door to Cassidy and Dad's bathroom and grabbed three bottles of pills from the medicine cabinet. I sorted through the prescriptions, gathered about twenty pills, and I swallowed every one. The next day, I awoke in a hospital bed, disappointed to find I was still alive and immediately given the *scare speech* from Cassidy. And then, without bothering to ask how I was feeling, she began *prepping* me on how to answer any questions about my overdose.

I later muddled off Cassidy's version of the incident to both the police and a social worker. I'd said I'd taken the pills by mistake. Which they were either too stupid or too oblivious to question.

Before I was discharged, the doctor said the combination of drugs I'd taken was enough to kill a horse. But for some reason, I'd survived. And to this day, I don't understand why.

Chapter
THIRTEEN

Ragan

January 16, 2017

THE RING-A-LING OF THE DOOR CHIME SIGNALS THE official start of my day. I stand in the entryway, my gaze fluttering over the space that within two weeks has already become too familiar. The 1950s rock-and-roll motif, the old-school jukebox bellowing the tunes of Chuck Berry's "Maybelline," black-and-white-checkered tile flooring, and themed seating areas all scream *Happy Days*. The only thing missing is Fonzie and his equally hot cousin Chachi.

I smooth down my felt poodle skirt and let out a breath, sending a silent prayer that today treats me better than yesterday. Scanning the dining area, I take in the regulars. Cassandra in the *Little Richard* booth slumped over her MacBook—more than likely OD'ing on caffeine as she cranks out her next article for the local paper. Ronnie at his usual table, gnawing at a corn cob. Mel at the counter, nursing a black coffee. The little old ladies from Aunt Sophie's church group sitting shoulder to shoulder in the *Elvis Presley* booth, eating muffins and sipping tea. And other familiar faces scattered throughout the space. It's uncanny. A place like this having regulars. Not that the diner is all that crummy, but other than the decades-old theme, it's nothing to write home about. Maybe that's why folks like it. It's not pretentious or overpriced. It's merely an extension of most homes here in Blue Ridge.

"Hey, Carrie," I say, giving my coworker a quick smile as I stroll past her to my locker.

"Happy Hump Day, Ragan," she says, all bright and bouncy as usual.

I don't see what's so *happy* about it. And as for humping, there's no *bumping* or *grinding* on my horizon unless I do it to my pillow. And call me crazy, but I don't find that too appealing.

I tie an apron around my waist, check for my pen and pad, then head back to the counter with perky-ass Carrie. Although I've come to genuinely like her, I'm so not in the frame of mind for perky today.

I guess she senses my mood because she dials it down a notch and we busy ourselves with prepping the silverware as she fills me in on her mama's bingo palooza night. I don't add much dialogue, just a nod or uh-huh here and there.

We fall into a routine of my placing a fork, spoon, and knife in the center of a napkin, and Carrie rolls the bundle and secures it with a paper ring. She doesn't seem to mind keeping the conversation going while I remain silent. She's yet to zip her lips and chatters away as we fold the remaining silverware into the napkins. Then midsentence, she suddenly falls quiet. I look up from the bundles to find her eyes pinned to the door, her bright red-coated lips partially spread.

"As I live and breathe. Look who just stepped into Jim Bob's Diner," she says, her voice a mix of awe and lust.

I follow her gaze and nearly choke, almost swallowing my gum. *Holy shit!* Is that…? No. It can't be. I squeeze my lids on a long blink. When I open my eyes, he's still there. The star of Blue Ridge… standing in Jim Bob's Diner. *Holy fucking shit! It's Branch McGuire.* Flanked by a group of muscle heads, just like in high school. And also just like in high school, Branch is hotter than all of them put together. And not the typical football player kind of hot. He's the make-you-come-just-by-standing-too-close kind of hot.

Branch is a pretty big deal in this town. Hell, he's a pretty big deal in *any* town. If anyone even mentions the word *football*, his name is close behind. He's that hot of a commodity, and given the overconfident swagger and cocksure set of his shoulders, he knows it. *No surprise there.*

He was a conceited asshat in high school and he's undoubtedly several times worse now. Nonetheless, I have to give credit where it's due. I follow the game enough to know the attention he receives on the field is well-deserved. With six Pro Bowls, MVP awards, record-breaking completion percentages, and most touchdown passes to date, he's one of the most sought-after quarterbacks in the NFL. According to a commentator from last week's game, Branch can write his ticket to any team in the league. So yeah, he's quite impressive, both on the field and off.

"Lord have mercy," Carrie whispers, fanning herself with one of Jim Bob's menus.

I glance at her again. She's practically bursting at the seams. Sometimes I forget she's married, and I have a feeling she does, too. I shake my head, watching as she adjusts her boobs in the low-cut shirt that hugs her frame a little bit more than what's acceptable for work. Jim Bob's almost daily reprimands about her so-called uniform have obviously fallen on deaf ears.

Carrie slides her tongue across her lip. "The things I'd do to that fine piece of man would get me arrested."

"What about *divorced*? How about that?" I ask. "Or is prison your only concern?"

She rolls her eyes and waves me off.

I turn my focus back to Branch, assessing each aspect of his appearance. The gray compression shirt that clings to every muscle of his chiseled torso. The short sleeves that reveal a portion of his tattoos. The trim waist. The loose gym shorts that commit the godawful act of underexposing the thick bands of muscle that run along his thighs.

So hot.

Too hot.

My eyes crawl up his body, only to repeat the same delicious trail downward again. This time, at a much slower pace, I take it all in… the face, the chest, the arms, the thighs… *everything*. Fucking gorgeous.

Branch works the crowd, grinning as he signs autographs and poses for pictures. All the while, my gaze remains firmly fixed on him—my heart hammering, my palms sweaty, my mouth bone dry. I wonder if I appear as shell-shocked as Carrie. *Fuck, I hope not.* But I sure as hell feel as if I do.

After acknowledging a few more admirers, and giving a brief statement to Cassandra for the paper, Branch and his boys walk toward one of the tables and take their seats. In *my* station. *Mine.*

Wait. What?

A surge of anxiety twists my stomach. I *cannot* serve Branch McGuire. I won't. I turn to Carrie, prepared to ask her to take my station, but one of her more impatient customers waves a hand, requesting his check, and she hurries off in his direction.

My eyes flash back to Branch and his buddies. The Quad. That's what they were known as back then. Each one of them hot, lewd, and egotistical. And leopards like that don't change their spots. Dealing with one of them would be a challenge. But all four? I'll take a hard pass. They're in *my* station though. And my shift is starting right now, so I can't very well take a break. I suppose I could ask Jim Bob to cover their table. I dismiss that thought almost as quickly as it popped into my head. No way would he do that for me, especially considering the number of free meals he's had to fork over because of my less-than-stellar skills as a waitress.

I catch a view of my appearance in the Coca-Cola mirror that doubles as a clock. And as expected, I look a mess—a few locks of hair tucked behind my ears and the rest in a Barbie ponytail gone wrong. Not that it matters. A guy like Branch won't do more than look right through me.

"Are you going to wait on that table or stand here staring at your reflection?" Jim Bob asks, having come to see what all the fuss is about—the noise in the diner is about ten decibels higher since Branch's arrival.

"Sorry," I say and grab four menus and take the reluctant steps toward the Quad.

"Welcome to Jim Bob's," I say when I come to a stop at their table and distribute the menus, keeping my head low, avoiding direct eye contact with any of them… especially

Branch. "Can I start you off with something to drink?"

"Beer," they say, almost in unison.

Kinda early for beer, but if it gives me a reason to place some distance between this group and me, I'll take it. "Look over the menus and I'll be right back with your drinks."

"Wait a minute, sugar."

Oh shit. It's Branch. I inhale a breath and turn, my gaze still cast downward as much as possible without looking too much like a total psycho.

"Aren't you going to look at me?" he asks.

I wasn't planning on it. I need to look up, to meet his gaze, but I stall. Will he recognize me? Will he remember that night? Then I realize someone as arrogant as Branch would never remember someone like me, so I lift my eyes to his.

Sweet fuck. I damn near swallow my gum again. As if he wasn't already emanating I-can-have-any-pussy-I-want vibes from a distance, being up close is like he's pulling your thighs apart, cupping your sex, and claiming it as his. Some men simply possess that type of power, and Branch is one of those men. It's kind of like when the citizens of Gotham cast the bat symbol—the criminals freak out and then Batman comes and does his thing. Well, in this case, Branch sends out *Man on Fire* signals and pussies in the immediate vicinity start to purr. And by purr, I mean wet panties. And by wet panties, I mean I'm gonna need to change mine after he leaves because my kitty is purring like a well-tuned engine on the motor speedway right about now. So yeah, he's definitely the make-you-come-just-by-standing-too-close kind of hot.

My eyes fall to the pad in my hand. *Stop it, Ragan. You can do this.* Meet his gaze. See what he wants, and step away from the cock. Yeah, I know he's more than cock, but when a pussy is purring the way mine is, that's all you can think of. Well, *that* and how to get a release. Suddenly, humping my pillow doesn't seem so far-fetched.

He's waiting. They all are. So look at him. *I can do that. Yes, I can do that.* Too bad I don't. On the way up, I get distracted, my gaze sliding over the biceps of his tattooed arm—his muscles are even bigger up close, and that poor shirt he's wearing doesn't stand a chance. It's practically a second layer of skin. *Holy shit, holy shit, holy shit.* Where is Carrie when I need her?

"My eyes are up here, sweetheart," Branch says, and the table erupts into laughter.

Ha ha ha. Very funny, asshat. As with most hot guys, it would appear Branch is much hotter with his mouth closed. I look up from where my eyes should not have been and swallow. *There goes my gum.*

His eyes caught me off guard. They're breathtaking. A brilliant blue. A *clear* blue. Like the close-up shots in the movies, the ones of the crystal clear waters of the Caribbean. Sure, like most of the world, I've seen Branch in magazines and on TV, but damn, they sure skimmed on the detail. I remember studying his features in high school, but they've matured over the years, his jawline more defined, his cheekbones more angular. His hair is still that dirty blond that matches his thick brows. And his eyes were always captivating, but now even more so. And those lips... just kill me now. They're the exact amount of plump to make a girl get lost in fantasies about how they'll feel pressed up against hers. All in all, the total package is positively mouthwatering. "Did you need something else?" I somehow manage to ask.

"Aren't you going to ask what kind of beer we want?"

"No," I reply, and glance down again, pretending to scribble something on my pad.

"And why is that?"

I force my eyes to meet his. "Because we only serve one kind. So it's Miller Lite or nothing."

He drops his menu and rears back in his seat, his eyes roaming over my face as if he's expecting something he didn't get.

"Is there a problem?" I ask, my attitude making an appearance to overshadow the insecurities.

"I was about to ask you the same question, darlin'."

First it was *sugar*. Then *sweetheart*. Now *darlin'*. I like it because those words slipping from his lips somersault my insides. I don't like it because I'm almost certain those are his generic pet names for all women. Well, not for me. "My name tag reads Ragan."

"Guess she told you, Branch," one of his buddies says and chuckles as the others join in on the laugh.

Branch throws a glance at them and his eyes are back on me, flashing a smile that squares his jaw. His lips spread over perfectly white teeth that could easily dazzle every woman in this diner all at once. And probably some of the guys, too, I figure, thinking of Ronnie, one of our regulars. Yeah, Branch would bedazzle the hell out of him.

Branch glances at my name tag and his eyes flash back to mine. For a long beat, there's nothing. He simply stares. But why? Does he remember me? Nah, that can't be it. Is he *into* me? That certainly isn't it. *Oh fuck. Say something already.* But he doesn't. So I stand there, my body prickling under his gaze. "Is there anything else? If not, I need to grab those beers."

With a shake of his head, he rakes his eyes over me again, taking in what I know is a disheveled heap that's only marginally passing as a waitress. Why, oh, why couldn't this have been Carrie's table?

"Branch, don't keep the girl waiting," Matt says.

He stares long enough to make me uncomfortable before he narrows his eyes and grins. "I'm done," Branch says as if dismissing me.

"I'll be right back with your drinks," I say and turn, heading toward the rear of the diner. *Finally.* Thank fuck. I have no idea what was running through his head. He was basically fucking with me because he could. And having me stand there when he clearly didn't want anything pissed me off, but it also made me think things I shouldn't. Like how it probably takes little to no conversation for him to get any woman naked.

"How did he smell?" Carrie whispers when I'm back behind the bar.

My brows scrunch. "What? I don't know. I didn't get close enough to *smell* him." But that's a lie. I *did*, and it was a raw woodsy musk that my body reacted to immediately. With his scent alone, he'd taken control of my bump-and-grind parts. My you-know-what is still clenching as if someone hit *vibrate* on a remote setting.

"Damn, I wanted that table," Carrie says, her eyes glued to the hot quarterback.

"Take it. It's yours."

"My shift is over and Tony's outside waiting on me. He has as much patience as a pecker getting its first piece of petunia."

"Lucky you," I say. "You get to leave."

"Now that's where you're wrong. I'd trade places with you in a heartbeat. Just to smell Branch McGuire's sweat," she says, her eyes stuck on the local football star, her gaze like that of the lovesick Pepe Le Pew.

"Go home and have sex with your husband and quit lusting over someone who's young enough to be your son."

"Sex is definitely on the menu tonight. And sure, I'll be holding on to Tony, but I'll be imagining those loose flabby arms of his are the nice, tight, firm muscles of Branch McGuire," she says, dotting her face with a napkin. "I'll get his autograph before I head out. That will make Tony less crabby about having to wait on me."

"Don't forget to lean in and get a good whiff of Branch's sweat," I say, jokingly but serious all at the same time.

"You're in the wrong profession, Ragan because you were reading my mind—that's exactly what I intend to do."

"You do know you're married, right?" I ask and place the last glass of beer on the tray.

"Yeah, but I ain't dead." She removes her apron and looks up at me. "And honey, where does it say I can't look or use my imagination? You need all the imagination you can muster when you're trapped underneath Tony."

I laugh and head back toward the four men who were undoubtedly going to make my next hour the most unbearable part of my day.

"Let me know how it goes."

"Won't be much to tell," I say, glancing over my shoulder.

"Watch out, Ragan!"

I spin around and before I know it, the tray goes flying and I'm on my ass. The glasses are in the air, and I'm looking up at the beer as it comes falling to the floor.

"Dammit." I lift my gaze, immediately finding Branch as his eyes flicker to mine. He looks at the mess I've made and returns his gaze to me, a slightly frustrated expression on his face.

Jim Bob dashes from behind the counter. "Are you all right?"

"Yeah, I'm fine." *Just embarrassed as hell.*

"Why is that mop bucket still here?" he asks, his face marred in a frown as he reaches to help me from the floor.

Oh my God. Why is this happening?

"I told you to move that thing after you clocked in."

"I'm sorry, Jim Bob."

"I'll clean this up," he says, looking over the broken glass and wasted liquor. "Go ahead and get some more beer for that table."

"Will do." I head back to the bar. *I can't believe that happened.* And now my reluctance to meet Branch's gaze increases tenfold.

I concentrate on placing the glasses on the tray and getting the beer over to the table. But it takes more effort than it should. "Sorry," I repeat as I walk past Jim Bob who's still cleaning up shattered glass and alcohol.

"This is coming out of your check, Ragan. You can't keep breaking all of my shit," he says, grumpy and low enough that only I can hear.

I let out a sigh as I move closer to Branch's table. "Here ya go." I place the glasses in front of each of the guys who are clearly amused by my fall.

Jerks.

"I suppose I should have warned you that stepping away from me wouldn't lessen the effect I have on you. But you need to be more careful, sugar," Branch says.

Aesthetically speaking, he is perfection. But yep, absolutely hotter with a closed mouth. "Trust me… that had nothing to do with you and everything to do with a mop bucket that was someplace it wasn't supposed to be."

He responds with a deep manly chuckle. "If you say so."

Biting my tongue, I turn away from the asshat who's pulling at my patience—*and my loins*—and face the others. "Have ya'll decided what you want?" I grab my pad and pen and take down their orders. After scribbling the last one, I tuck my pen behind my ear. "If that's all, I'll get those out to you in a few."

"Try not to drop it this time, darlin'," Branch says. "We're in a hurry."

"Yeah, and I'll try not to spit on it either, *darlin'*," I mumble, the guys snickering as I step away.

Chapter
FOURTEEN

Branch

January 16, 2017

"S O YOUR PHONE *DOES* WORK?" IT'S MORE OF AN accusation than a question.

"Er… hello? Branch, is that you?"

"Yeah," I reply, apprehension already creeping in.

"It's… er… good to hear from you. I have to say I'm shocked though."

"Can't be any more shocked than I am that you answered."

"You're my son. Why wouldn't I answer?"

"Jace called you a few days ago." *He's your son, too, but you sure as fuck didn't answer.*

"Er… yeah. About that. I'd planned to call him, but I got busy and it slipped my mind. Is everything all right?"

This guy. Fucking typical. "Had you given a damn, you'd know the answer to that question."

"Let's not start this, Branch. You know good and well why things are the way they are."

"Is this the part where you blame Mama again?"

"If history has taught me anything, it's that conversations about Mary never end well. I don't like to go down that road with you boys."

My fingers curve around the phone and I fight the urge to hang up.

After an extended silence he asks, "Are you still there?"

I swallow the anger that's clawing its way to the surface. "I'm in town. We need to talk."

"Oh… uh… okay. I'd like that," he says, the shock sifting through the phone. "It would be great to see you. How long has it been, Branch?"

"I don't know. I stopped keeping track seven or eight years ago."

"Son, I—"

"I'll be at the garage tomorrow at noon."

"At Jimmy's?" he asks, the hesitation apparent in his voice. "I think we should meet someplace else, don't you? Why not come by the house? Meet your brother. Say hi to your step-sister. And Charlene—she'd love to see you."

Yeah, and Mama will have a fucking coronary if she ever finds out. But that's not the reason I won't go. "Will you be there or not?"

He's quiet for a beat and finally says, "As long as Jimmy is cool with it… I am, too."

"Jimmy's cool. Jimmy's always cool."

"Well, okay. I guess I'll see you tomorrow then. And Branch?"

"Yeah?"

"I know I said it already, but I'm glad you called. It's been too long, son."

"Yeah. Sure." I hang up and meet the eyes of Dad's former

best friend.

He slaps me across the shoulder. "I'm proud of you. That's a big step."

I shrug off his words. "Haven't done anything yet."

Jimmy doesn't say another word, but I'm sure he knows where my head is. On my parents. And on the hell they made of the McGuire household. My thoughts flash to the brief phone call—to Dad's words of not *going down that road*. Not only did he avoid the road, he avoided the whole damn vicinity.

Sure, he made the effort… for a while. But then his visits to the house stopped. I couldn't tell if that made Mama better or worse. Or how the hell they managed to get past their bullshit long enough to create Jace. That one is still a mystery to me. They'd been apart for years, argued for years—before, during, and after the divorce. They *never* got along, at least not in front of me. So when she told me she was pregnant, I was floored. And I had questions. *How long had it been going on? Did it mean they were getting back together? Or did they just fall into a moment of weakness? And where the hell did Charlene filter into all of it?* Never figured out what the hell any of it meant because Mama would never answer my questions, and despite the pregnancy, things didn't get better. The downward spiral continued.

More arguments, more of what I thought at the time were Mama's *crazy woman days*, and more struggles to make ends meet. Days without electricity, days when the water was off, and days when breakfast, lunch, and dinner consisted of peanut butter and jelly sandwiches. Not sure why dear old Dad figured it was cool to withhold financial support, but he did. And that was around the time I started working more hours with Jimmy.

Those were hard times. Times I want to forget, but can't. Times that—to this day—shape my views about money. You'd have to live under a rock to *not* know who I am, but on the off chance you didn't, you'd often think I was a typical Joe Schmo who worked a nine to five, living check to check. But then there are cases when my status speaks for itself— the NFL career, the luxury penthouse, the fancy sports cars, and over-the-top parties. But that's not my everyday mentality. Although I have a shitload of money now, it's not easy to shake off what I grew up living every day. So for the most part, I live rather conservatively. My money is saved, invested, and diversified. Because there's not a day that goes by that I don't remember where I came from and how I intend to never go back.

I've made provisions to ensure Mama and Jace will always be taken care of. They'll never see the dark days of peanut butter and jelly sandwiches. As for Dad, I honestly don't give a fuck. For years I've figured that ran both ways, but something in his tone has planted a seed of doubt that I can't shake.

The crew breaks for lunch, leaving Jimmy and me in the garage. And at the top of the hour, in walks the guy I can barely stand the sight of.

I'm in the same room with the man who gave me life. *Curtis McGuire.* My father. Unwillingly, I study him. He's almost unrecognizable. The lines etched in his face show signs of the years between us. He's heavier, at least twenty pounds or so. And he's sporting a beard, a full beard.

I let the shock settle, only to open myself to the more familiar emotion—the anger that's always lying idle in my chest.

"You look good, son."

I tip my chin. "Dad."

"Hey, Jimmy," he says, reaching out to shake his hand.

"Good to see ya, Curtis," Jimmy says. His exchange is genuine, verifying what I've questioned for years—he misses his best friend.

"Can you imagine? My boy. *The Man on Fire*."

"He's something else, all right," Jimmy says. "You should be proud."

"I am," Dad says, looking back at me. "There aren't enough words." He extends his arms. "Branch. Son, can I—"

I take a few paces back. "Can you what?"

"Give you a hug?" he asks, closing the space between us.

"I'm not here for any father-son moments."

Dad drops his hands, and his sideward glance at Jimmy says he's embarrassed.

"So another kid, huh?" I ask.

He gives a proud smile. "Yeah, you have a new baby brother. Curtis, Jr. I'd like for you boys to meet him."

"I don't think so, Pops."

"Branch, I'm trying here, but are you gonna keep shooting me down? And I'll be honest, I don't know where to start with a son I've had nothing but a one-sided media relationship with for the past fifteen years. But I was hoping your call meant you were ready to meet me halfway. Was I wrong?"

"That call had nothing to do with me. This is about Jace. He's gonna need you to step up. As a parent."

"Is Mary all right?" he asks.

I shake my head. "Man, don't pretend as if you give a damn."

"Now wait a minute, Branch. You got no right claiming to know how I feel."

"If you felt anything at all, she wouldn't be like she is now."

"I didn't do anything to that woman."

I take an involuntary step toward him. "*That woman*? That's all she is to you now?"

"Branch, I'm tired of being painted as the bad guy in all of this."

"Are you saying the state you left her in is the state you found her in? That you aren't responsible for supplying her with the drugs that fucked her head up?"

"I'm saying she made her own damn choices!" His voice rises. "Same as I did."

"You need to take some responsibility for what you did to her!"

"That was of *her* doing. She did what she wanted. She asked for something and I gave it to her."

"You lying piece of crap." I rush him, my hand fisting his shirt as I shove his body against the wall, my knuckles inches from his face.

"Go ahead. Hit me! If that's gonna make you feel better, do it!"

Yeah, it'll go a long way toward making me feel better. Knocking the hell out of him is long overdue.

"Branch, beating the shit out of Curtis won't erase any of the memories… or the pain," Jimmy says.

I pull my eyes away from Dad and look over at Jimmy. He takes a step closer, his empathetic gaze flush with mine. "It won't give back anything you've missed. And it won't fix Mary."

Jimmy's said all he plans to, and he won't physically restrain me from a fight that I want. But in his eyes, I see the words he won't speak. He wants me to handle this like a man, not like a scorned kid. I'm pretty familiar with all of Jimmy's expressions. I know when he wants me to choose for myself. I know when he wants me to do the right thing. And I know when he's disappointed in me. This look is a combination of all three.

I turn back toward Dad. "You should have been there, dammit!" I explode. "You should have fucking showed up." I release my grasp of his shirt and my fist goes through the drywall. Jimmy and Dad say nothing.

Knocking the fuck out of Curtis McGuire won't change shit, but it sure as fuck won't hurt. Jimmy's right, though. It's pointless. It won't erase the days I sat outside the school and waited for Dad. It won't expunge memories of the game nights I scanned the bleachers hoping to see his face, or the banquet dinners with the other parents, where Jimmy and Loretta always filled in for mine. Or the times I sat in the park and watched him with his other family. And it won't fix the mess he left behind for me to clean up.

"Don't you think I wanted to be there?" Dad asks, the impassioned tone of his voice forcing me to take pause. "Everything I tried, Mary made it impossible. That's why I stopped coming to the house. But I thought, hey, I can go to the school, meet up with Branch there. Maybe hang out with him before practice and stick around for a while and watch him do his thing. But you know what? The first time I did that, your mama somehow caught wind of it. And so she made a point of showing up every day after school."

He stops briefly, taking in my expression. "I see it on your face. You remember, don't you?"

I do, but I won't say. I look at him, confusion combating the anger.

"And there was that one time when she showed her ass, *literally*, to your whole damn team. Do you remember that? Do you remember how humiliated you were? Do you think I wanted that for you? To be the laughingstock? So then I figured, I'd go to your away games. Back then, Mary hated sports and I figured she wouldn't go through the trouble, but guess what? She was there, too. That woman was determined to make it impossible for me to be the kind of father to you that I wanted to be. So I stopped trying. I didn't want any more images in your head that you couldn't get rid of, so I prayed the good memories you had of me were better than the ones she'd smear... and I stayed away. And I was hoping you'd give me the chance to explain one day—that you'd somehow understand."

I see the plea in his eyes, desperate for my belief in him. And as much as I don't want to admit it, I know he's telling the truth. And it hits me hard. As though someone has jabbed me in the gut. I sit on the stool beside Jimmy in the garage. With nothing to say, I place my hands on the worktable and open the toolbox. Dad follows me and goes on, telling me things I'm not sure I want to hear.

"I loved your mother, Branch. I did. And I would've stayed with her until the end of time. But she didn't want that. She didn't want *me*. She stopped looking at me like she used to. She stopped loving me," he says. His voice breaks on his last couple of words, and I'm left dumbfounded because nothing he says lines up with what Mama has convinced me of over the years.

I study him, absorbing the shock of his words. There's a faraway look in his eyes as he travels back in time to a place that I can see causes him pain. It's difficult *not* to see it.

"You have no idea—and I pray you never will—how it feels to look into the eyes of a woman you love more than your own life and know she thinks you're less than nothing."

My gaze flickers to Jimmy's and he appears as confounded as I.

"And it wasn't only that. I had it in me to fight my way back to her. And I would have, but there's only so much a man can take." He shakes his head and his gaze clouds with visions of the past. "The constant belittling. Day in, day out. All the arguing and yelling. And the fights. They became worse. They'd get louder and louder, and Mary would start throwing things, so I'd leave the house for a while. When it got to the point where I wanted to retaliate or where it was something I was afraid you'd see, I knew it was time to leave." He shakes his head. "My sticking around wasn't good for anyone, especially for you."

I remember those days and some of the nights. I'd go to my room, put on my headphones, and drown the noise out.

"I suppose I could have fought for sole custody, and maybe I should have, but I didn't have the heart to take you from your mama. Despite her issues, I knew how much she loved you. But once you were out of the house, I tried to reach out, to forge a relationship with you, but you wouldn't hear of it. I guess you thought I only wanted to be in your life because you'd made it big." Dad looks away for a moment, then directly at me. "But son, I didn't want a dime of your money. I didn't give a damn about the fame. I wanted my son back. I wanted to play a few rounds of catch with you like I did when you were a kid. I wanted to go on those fishing trips we'd planned." His hand rests on my shoulder with a reassuring squeeze. "I wanted to tell you how proud I am... how proud I've always been of you."

Those words hang in the air—*I'm proud of you.* The words I've always wanted to hear, that every son wants to hear from his father. And now that I've finally heard them—fifteen years too late—does it even matter?

He turns to Jimmy. "You were wrong about Charlene and me. Nothing was going on beyond having someone to listen. Someone to appreciate me. We'd talk and hang out a bit. But that's all it was. You and Loretta had such a great thing going. I was maybe even a little jealous. You had what I wanted with Mary. And I was too embarrassed to tell you how messed up things were at home. That Mary didn't see me as a man anymore. So when you—the one person who knew me better than anyone—accused me of something I would have never done, it pushed me over the edge. You kept at it and then one day, after a blowup with Mary, it struck a nerve." His face tightens into a grimace. "Sorry for throwing that first punch. That never should have happened."

Jimmy looks at Dad with a seemingly new understanding. "I didn't know. I wish I could have—"

"No. That was all me. And thank you for being there for my boys when I couldn't be."

Jimmy nods.

"If you're up to it, I'd like to catch up. Maybe grab a beer with ya sometime."

"You have my number," Jimmy says, reaching out for Dad's hand.

Dad pulls him into a full hug and I know their friendship is on the mend. Something I never saw coming.

Curtis leaves the garage, unburdened by the load he carried all these years, but the words he aired remain, and they circle round and round my head. I'm regrouping and rethinking everything I thought I knew. I recover from his revelation only to replay it over and over, pacing across the floor of Jimmy's office. I try to sort through truths and lies to see if there are any holes in Dad's story, something he's left out or even misrepresented, but I don't see it. All I see is what he's told me, and though I don't want it to, it all makes sense. I've gone most of my life thinking he checked out on us. On *me*. But now I question it all.

He told me how it all started with his shoulder injury. About his rehab and how it was as much mental as it was physical, and while he had the physical part covered, the mental part was being broken down at home. Mama rode him every day about getting better. She got in his head, added pressure, and he swore that it stifled his recovery. The absence of support from a spouse can be the blow that destroys you and your career. I've seen it with a few players. Not only that, it was my theory that women get in your head if they hang around too long, which is why one night is all I bother with. I get in, I get out, and I'm done. Anything more is a risk I'm not willing to take.

Dad's shoulder never returned to its preinjury state and he was eventually cut from the team. His career as a semi-professional football player was over.

He later grew to resent Mama, even blaming her for the turn their lives took. But that resentment went both ways. Mama blamed Dad for it all, claiming she would have chosen a different life had she not been seduced by his pie-in-the-sky dreams.

I remember her telling me that Grandma warned her about Dad, saying he would end up *a nobody*, that she chose the wrong man. I guess Mama finally bought into it and that's when she coined a phrase that has become as familiar to me as Nike's *Just Do It* slogan—*I could have been somebody. I could have married Nathanial Barnes.* I don't know who the hell Nathanial Barnes is, but after Dad's disclosure, I have to ask the questions he undoubtedly asked himself. How many times can a man hear that he's nothing more than a consolation prize before he removes himself from the picture altogether? And how many times can he come home to a wife who doesn't appear to want him there at all?

He said that every day, another piece of him was nicked off, and it became increasingly difficult to step into a house that had become a battlefield. So coming in later and later was the temporary solution... until he eventually stopped coming home altogether.

After that, Dad managed to drop by to see me a few days out of the week. But the run-ins with Mama decreased those visits to a once-a-week Sunday dinner, until those stopped, too. Every dinner was awkward. There was always that something in the air that warned me to brace myself for what was coming. *And it always came.* There wasn't one visit they didn't end up at each other's throats.

As for the handful of times Dad arranged scheduled

weekends with me, Mama made it damn near impossible for me to leave. What should have been a step out of the house and into Dad's car became an event met with yelling, foul language, and accusations just to get me out the door—giving the neighbors a front-row seat to our dysfunction. And when I was back home, Mama guilted me for *abandoning* her to spend time with *one of the worst fathers in the world.*

Everything else Dad revealed this afternoon leaves me without words. Everything I've grown up believing has been a lie. Some things that never added up now make sense, while other details become a source of confusion... and condescension. Every reason I had for hating him was fabricated. And when I asked about the lack of financial support, he delivered a blow that obliterated *everything* else. Things that can only be explained by Mary McGuire.

I'm not sure where Dad and I stand now. But for the first time in as long as I can remember, I don't hate him. Maybe I never did—same as Mama. Dad may have thought she stopped loving him, but I know different.

If anything positive resulted from the conversation, it was Dad's commitment to being present in Jace's life. I believed him. I saw the eagerness. I saw the anticipation as he ticked off ideas of how they would spend time together. I had the feeling some of those things were from the list he'd made for him and me. And that tugged at my gut, reminding me of how much I missed out on with my dad. But this time, I'm not angry at him. That feeling is replaced with another emotion I can't yet identify. I even gave him the hug he asked for. And then, with wet eyes, he walked away, leaving me to take the next step.

I don't know what or if there will be a next step, but I got what I needed from this meeting. Dad promised to step up and be the father Jace will need. And I told him I'll make sure Mama allows him to be there for Jace—that I'll make sure she behaves. He was skeptical that she would. Hell, so am I.

Chapter
FIFTEEN

Ragan

January 17, 2017

"**G**UESS WHO GOT SOME LAST NIGHT?" CARRIE adjusts her neckerchief, giving her cleavage the attention she feels it so richly deserves.

I cover the freshly baked cookies with a lid and slide the carousel to the far end of the counter. "So Tony did you up real good, huh?"

"He sure did. And my thoughts of a certain you-know-who helped with a second round this morning." She winks with a wicked little grin.

I roll my eyes at her insinuation. "Oh God. Don't tell me you were thinking of—"

"Hell yeah, I was. And it was *incredible*. I wonder how long he's in town for," she says, leaning on the counter, propping up on her elbows, and exhaling a blissful sigh.

I've been wondering the same. I mean, how can anyone *not* want more of that, even if he is a bit of an asshat. "After yesterday, I doubt he steps in here again."

"Was it that bad?"

"Worse."

Carrie frowns. "Like *bad service, but still get a tip* kinda worse or *no tip at all* kinda worse?"

"He dropped three twenties and told me to keep the change. Considering the check was almost sixty bucks, I'd say *no tip at all* kinda worse."

Her lips curl into a sympathetic smile. It's more on the side of pity than sympathy, but self-pity is sitting so heavy on me these days it doesn't faze me in the least.

"You need to work on that shit, Ragan. Jim Bob fired the last girl because of that."

"Yeah, he's mentioned it ten or a billion times between deducting from my check."

"Today's a new day, and I'm here with you all afternoon, so I'll help you out as much as I can." She flicks her gaze over the dining area. "Let's get this place hopping, shall we?" She sifts her retro ponytail through her fingers and heads for the jukebox. "What are you in the mood for, my friend?"

I shrug. "Surprise me."

Seconds later, we're laughing, dancing, and singing along to "Rock Around The Clock."

Jim Bob steps from the back, tips his head to Carrie, but flashes a warning my way. "I don't want any problems out of you today, Ragan."

"Yes, sir." *I'll be fine as long as I don't have to serve hot-as-fuck asshats named Branch McGuire.*

"I'm only keeping you on as a favor to your folks," he continues. "Anyone else would have been long gone by now."

I don't reply aloud but can't help my inward response. *How will I ever repay you, Mr. Jim Bob Higgins for allowing me to stay on at this fine establishment? For giving me the opportunity to continue serving this five-star cuisine?* Fucker.

I laugh aloud at my inner monologue as Jim Bob looks on, probably wondering if I've lost my marbles. "Thanks, Jim Bob," I manage to say with a straight face. "I'm sure I'll get the hang of it. I mean, how many more orders can I possibly get wrong?"

He shakes his head, opens the register, and places the cash tray into the bottom.

Guessing that's my cue to get to work, I turn toward the dining area right as the door swings open. "Oh shit."

"What is it?" Carrie asks.

I tip my head toward the entrance.

"Ohhh, yeah. *Mr. Man on Fire* is back. I guess he missed me as much as I missed him," she whispers, holding her crossed fingers toward the heavens and offering a plea. "Please let him go to one of my tables. *Please.*"

I hope he does, too… but it doesn't happen. He heads right back to the same table as yesterday. "Damn," I curse under my breath.

"I can take that station if you take mine," Carrie offers.

I look toward Jim Bob as he closes the register, a frown marring his chubby face as he glances between Carrie and me.

"I'd better do it myself. You know Jim Bob isn't too happy with me right now."

"Well, holler if you need any help. We don't want a repeat of yesterday," she says.

I square my shoulders and head over to Branch, thankful he's flying solo yet still mentally preparing myself for another round of everything that happened the day before. "Welcome to Jim Bob's. Can I start you off with something to drink?" I ask and place a menu in front of him.

"Water," he says, without looking at me.

"Do you know what you're having today?"

He glances up from the menu but doesn't place his order. He does that staring thing—like before—as if he's waiting on something. Another apology for yesterday's service? Well, that ain't happening.

Yesterday was yesterday. Today's today. So his previous dining experience at Jim Bob's wasn't so great. In retrospect, it could've been much worse. So I got two of the orders wrong. No big deal. That sort of thing happens all the time. And so I mixed up steak sauce with hot sauce. Anyone in a hurry can grab the wrong bottle. Somehow I scribbled an order as *well done* instead of *medium well*. But in my defense, if they weren't all flapping their jaws at the same time as I was writing, maybe that one wouldn't have happened. Now, spilling the water in Matt's lap... that one was all me. But hey, mistakes happen in busy diners every day.

And Branch's time here couldn't have been that bad if he's back already. Besides, he and his childish friends taunted me the entire time. So in my book, that makes us even. Yeah, I was embarrassed, but I was also pissed. I came damn close to telling all four of them to fuck off, but that would have been my last day working for Jim Bob. And I need this job.

Somehow I made it through my previous shift without walking out and without getting fired, but here Branch is again today. Looking just as hot as he did yesterday, and judging from his demeanor, he's ready for a repeat performance. Thing is, I don't know if I can handle his shit two days in a row. Either he's about to give as good as he gets or I'm walking out.

"What's good?" he asks.

"I don't know. I never eat here," I lie.

"So maybe you should tell me the specials then."

I point to the chalkboard near the entrance. "Take your pick."

"Anyone ever tell you that you need to work on your disposition? I'm sure you'll get more tips if you do."

"Anyone ever tell you that you're a pain in the ass?" It slipped out before I could stop myself.

He grins. "Quite a few women actually. But they like it that way."

My mouth falls agape and my mind is pushed into a scene with my poodle skirt bunched around my waist, my panties slid to the side, and my torso bent over one of Jim Bob's tables as Branch McGuire takes me as long and as hard as he pleases. Heat rushes my cheeks as the image centers in my brain. *Oh, sweet baby Jesus.* Looks like I'm in for a different kind of torment today. *Focus, Ragan. His comment was rude and you should respond appropriately. And you're pissed at him, remember?* Right. That's right, I am. I tell kitty to stop purring and fall into the role of the *offended* waitress. "You didn't just say that."

He shrugs. "Well, you asked a question. I gave you an answer." He angles his head, and his eyes narrow as if he's trying to figure me out. "Should I have lied? Maybe you respond better to lies than you do to the truth. Most women are like that, you know."

This guy really is an asshat. "Maybe it's just the women *you* attract."

"Maybe." He places the menu on the table, his gaze unrelenting as he studies me. "But I'm sure you'd like it, too."

Oh my God. What the hell is he doing? He's fucking with me, right? Yeah, he is. Don't respond. Don't respond. *And kitty, please oh please stop purring.*

His gaze moves over me in a slow crawl, almost as if he's undressing me with his eyes. I shift on my feet, uncomfortable by what I think he sees.

"I don't imagine you get out much."

"And that concerns you, how?" I ask, already slighted by his assumption.

"You're not very friendly and you don't seem too concerned about your appearance." He breaks off and glances a few tables over, Carrie's you'd-better-leave-me-a-huge-tip laughter floating across the diner. She flashes a big, flirty smile at Branch and my eyes dart back to him in time to see him respond to her by raising his chin. "Maybe you should take some pointers from her?"

"Oh, so because I'm not pushing my boobs in your face or circling you like a dog in heat, I don't care about my appearance? Maybe next time, you should sit in *her* station. Problem solved."

A faint smile turns his lips. "Did I strike a nerve?"

"Why are you here again today anyway?" I ask, ignoring his question. "Didn't you have enough of dealing with me yesterday?"

"Just doing my part to support the local economy. Do you have a problem with that?"

"Why don't you just write a check? Isn't that what your kind does?" I know I should zip my lip, but if he isn't doing it, why should I?

"*My kind*?" He appears puzzled by my less-than-awestruck responses to him. "What's your deal, sugar?"

"Excuse me? My *deal*?"

"Do you *not* know who I am?"

I know exactly who you are. I'm pretty sure everyone in this diner knows who you are. And kitty definitely knows who you are. "You're a patron, like the others who come here. Place an order, eat, and leave. The only difference is you insist upon giving me a hard time."

"Trust me, darlin'. When I give you a hard time, you'll know it."

A mix of lust and embarrassment heats my cheeks as my mind flips back to the table scene. To the hot, mind-blowing, orgasm-inducing table scene. *Holy shit. Why me?*

"Did I say something that bothers you or did I say something you like?"

"Neither," I say and decide to give him what he wants. "And yes, I know you're *the* Branch McGuire. Is that what you want to hear?"

"If you know who I am, then what's your problem?"

"Oh, pardon me. Did I skip the part where I was supposed to drool and ask for your autograph?"

He laughs. "Well… yeah."

"Are you seriously admitting to that?"

He winks at me. "It's the truth. Sugar, I'm the hottest thing coming, and you know it."

"Sorry to disappoint you. I'm not a football fan," I lie. "And arrogance is a real turnoff for me, so why don't you skip this little dance and tell me what you want to eat, *sugar*."

He sits back and crosses his arms over his chest, his biceps testing the compression of his shirt. *Oh, to touch that arm.*

I lift my gaze and exhale an impatient sigh when he doesn't reply. "It's going to be a pretty busy hour, so if you don't want anything—" I cast my eyes toward the door chime and then back to Branch.

"The house salad, no dressing. Turkey burger, grilled with onions, no seasoning, tomato and lettuce, no bun."

I scribble his order on my pad.

"Do I need to repeat that? You know… to make sure you got it right this time?"

I look up to see him grinning at me. Yes, he's doing this again—having fun at my expense. My eyes drift back to the door and I shake my head at the happy-go-lucky girl walking toward me. She stops in her tracks when she notices Branch. Her eyes widen and dart back to me.

"Is she a friend of yours?" he asks.

"Yes."

"Ask her to come over."

"Why? Because in a matter of a second, she's already given you more of the reaction you like?"

"I'd like to meet her."

"I have a better idea. Let's pretend I'm a good waitress. Bright, perky, friendly, displaying the right amount of boobage… you know, the type who cares about her appearance. And let's say I take your order and surprise, surprise I get it one hundred percent accurate. You eat your meal. You leave a *decent* tip this time, and then we both go about our day. How about that?"

He rears back. An amused smile traces his lips.

"So instead of arranging your meet and greet, I'll focus all my brain cells on getting your order right. Don't want you disappointed two days in a row." I turn to leave but stop short. "And if you want to meet my friend, try waving her over yourself."

Chapter
SIXTEEN

Branch

January 22, 2017

I SPEND THE DAYS AND MOST OF THE NIGHTS INSIDE MY head. The quiet storm brewing. My mind connecting dots and erasing lines. My emotions ranging from anger and sadness to regret and confusion. My identity shaken.

Who the fuck am I if not the protector of Mary and Jace? If not the fatherless son who's spent a lifetime building walls and suppressing emotions. If not the player who doesn't want for anything beyond status, a payday, and a warm body whenever the mood strikes? And then, as if on a loop, I cycle through it all over again.

Dad's story has shaken the very foundation of who I am. Of the man I've become. Of the asshole who rides shotgun with the prodigal son. I wonder who I would've been. Who I could have become with both parents—as fucked up as they may be—in my life.

And then I ask the question that's on repeat. *What has Mama done?*

And an even better question…
Why?

The drive home is quiet.

Today's my first time seeing or speaking to Mama since before the game… since my talk with Dad. And that's a good thing because I've been fighting my way through a whirlwind of emotions, none of them good.

"Branch, is everything all right?"

"Yeah," I reply, staring straight ahead. "So the nurse will be working full-time at the house."

"Oh," she says. "Well, all right, but I don't think that's necessary. I haven't felt this good in years. But if you think it's best…"

No argument? Shocker.

"Well, is it Deidra?" she asks, the anticipation audible in her voice. "You know… the one I told you I liked?"

"No."

Mama falls quiet, and just as my mind settles into the silence, she says, "Don't tell me it's that Christina."

"Fine. I won't tell you then."

"But I told you—"

"She's familiar with your case and she already knows us."

"Yes, but—"

"She stays, Mama." I don't know if I went against her wishes because of the logic or because I wanted to punish her. Something tells me it's the latter.

"What's gotten into you, Branch? So cold and unyielding. You only behave this way when I've done something you don't approve of, but I've been good. Taking my meds without being coerced. Been nice to that know-it-all Dr. Blake and all of the hospital staff."

"That's acceptable and *expected* behavior, but as usual, you sound as though it's something that should be applauded."

I unlock the door and we step into the house.

Mama draws a breath and exhales. "Feels good to be home." When she turns and notices I haven't moved, her smile fades. "I may be a little off-kilter, but I know my son. Something's not right with you. What's going on?"

I wasn't planning to do this now, but since she asked... "All those years ago, why were you so opposed to my seeing Dad? Even now... why?"

Her gaze flicks over my face, and I catch the panic in her eyes. "You know why. You've always known why."

"Tell me again."

"Branch, I just walked through the door. I haven't seen Jace, and you've barely said one word to me. I want to catch up with my boys. Enjoy you for the time I have you. Why would I want to ruin my homecoming talking about a man who's wronged this family?"

"See, that's just it." I tilt my head to the side, my eyes narrowing as I study her reaction. "I don't think he's the one who wronged this family. I think it was you."

"Me?" Her eyes widen in shock and disbelief. "I'm the parent who didn't leave, remember?"

"Okay, let's start there. Why?"

"Why what?"

"Why did Dad leave?"

"You were here. You saw how things were."

"And why were they like that? What was your part in it?"

Her shoulders rise in a shrug. "Couples fight. Your father and I were no different."

When we hear a sound at the door, we turn, watching as it swings open. "Mama! You're home." Jace, clad in a soiled uniform, rushes toward us, bypassing me and going straight to Mama.

She pulls him into a hug. "Yep, I'm back."

"And you're all better?" he asks.

Mama throws a cautious glance toward me and says, "I sure am. So what have you been up to since I've been gone?"

"It's been a lot of fun. Branch took me fishing. We watched movies in the game room with Cory, Drake, and Sam. He's helped the coaches on my team and he even made homework fun. He's the best big brother."

"Yes, he is. He's a pretty great son, too. Just like you," she says and tousles his hair.

Jace turns toward me. "We should celebrate Mama coming home. Don't you think?"

"Uh… yeah, sure, little bro. Why don't you get cleaned up and we can all go out for dinner?"

When Jace leaves the room, I step closer to Mama and offer a warning. "You have tonight. But tomorrow, we will talk and you *will* answer my questions."

Mama and I sit on the backyard patio, the wind chimes filling the intermittent silence. I've asked question after question about Dad, only to have her dodge each one. I can see it's going to be like pulling teeth, so I get to the point. "Dad said he paid child support. According to him, he never missed a month. So what happened? Why did you say different? Why did you make me think he didn't give a damn?"

She lets out a frustrated sigh, shaking her head. "I can't believe you spoke to that man and let him fill your head with lies. What have I always told you?"

"Apparently not as much as you should have."

"Well, you can't trust a word that comes out of Curtis's mouth. He'll place the blame for everything on me and I won't have it. You are to stay away from him. Same goes for Jace."

"Mama, I don't have time for your manipulation. Especially since I don't know when or if you're gonna flip back to the *other* you."

The hurt of my words reflects in her eyes, yet she says nothing.

I exhale an impatient sigh. "Mama, I'm waiting. What happened to the money? Why did Dad leave?"

She places her coffee cup on the patio table and tugs at the collar of her shirt. "Air... I need air."

"Mama, you're outside. How much more air can you need?"

"Well, I feel as though I'm suffocating." She lays her palm flat on her forehead. "Something feels wrong. Maybe the new meds aren't working after all."

"Last night, you said you haven't felt so good in years," I offer in rebuttal.

"Yes, but maybe I spoke too soon. Maybe I need to—"

"You're wearing my patience. Stop with the diversion tactics and tell me the truth. Now, Mama."

"Branch, I've told you all I can remember. I don't know what you want from me."

"Okay, if that's how you want to play this." I pull out my phone and scroll through the contacts.

"What are you doing? Who are you calling?"

"I'm asking Dad to come over. See if he can help connect the dots." I press the call button and bring the phone to my ear.

"Hang up that phone, Branch. Right this minute!"

"I want answers and if you won't give them to me, I'm sure he'll be happy to."

"Fine! Fine! You want to know, I'll tell you. Your father left because of me!"

I push end on the call and shift my gaze to hers.

"Because I broke our vows. Because I became the person he hated to see at the end of the day. I knew I was wrong, but I didn't care. I kept at it. I wanted him to hate me because it made it easier for me to hate *him*."

What the hell? Broke her vows. Dad never mentioned anything about Mama breaking vows.

"Truth is… your father was a good man, a great father, and a saint of a husband."

"Then why keep me away from him?"

"Because I knew I was wrong!" she shouts. "For running him off. For breaking my commitment to him. And I figured if you knew the truth—that I was this shallow bitch of a person who'd run your daddy off—you'd choose him over me and I'd be left alone."

"You kept us apart so I wouldn't find out you caused the divorce? There has to be more to this story."

"When he left—something I didn't think he'd ever do—I

was devastated but too proud to ask him back. And when I found out he'd taken up with that whore, Charlene, that he'd gone straight from my bed to hers, it was bad, Branch. Really bad. I was hurt and I wanted him to hurt. And I figured the only way to do that was through you."

I shake my head, watching as life-altering words slip from her lips. "Do you realize what you've done? How fucked this all sounds?"

"It wasn't *all* me. It was the sickness."

My brows rise. "The sickness? You mean the one you swear you don't have?"

"Branch, please don't be this way."

I place my hands on the table, leaning in. "What kind of parent does that? Turns a child against their father to satisfy their own spiteful vengeance?"

"A shitty one. A screwed-up one, Branch. Isn't that what you're thinking?"

"Don't waste your energy playing that fucking card! It's not gonna work. Not this time."

"Branch, please try to understand," she says, quickly re-calculating her approach.

"Understand what? What you took from Dad? How you hijacked a significant part of my childhood? How you're doing the same damned thing to Jace?"

"You have to know that part of this was due to my mental issues, don't you? It wasn't all me," she says, desperation flashing across her face. "I wasn't always like this, Branch. Needing medication to keep my head on right. I was fine until Curtis left."

I sit back in the chair, trying to put everything together. "Until he left? Then where did the drugs come in?"

"There were never any hard drugs… just pot," she says, looking away as if embarrassed. "One evening, after one of our fights, Curtis went outside to get away from me. Me being me, I followed him and tried to kick-start round two, but he was completely unaffected by my taunts. He just took another drag and said, 'Whatever, Mary.' I poked and jabbed but with each word, he became more and more lax. And that's when I remembered what he'd told me. That Mary Jane made the fast *slow* and the important *trivial.* In that moment, that was exactly what I needed—slow and trivial, so I asked him to let me try it. And to my surprise, I liked it, liked the way it made me feel. I was calm and more like the person I wanted to be, so I told him I needed my own stash. I figured I'd have it on standby for those days when I couldn't seem to turn myself off. I'm sure that was music to his ears. A calm Mary McGuire didn't come around often. Anyway, he came home one night and pulled out an extra bag of pot for me. And I never touched it until the day he moved out. The following morning, I felt weird. Like I was floating from one scene to the next. Been feeling weird ever since."

My eyes are pinned to the martyred expression in hers. And I try to picture Mama as she described. As an innocent. But the hue of righteous indignation won't let me. I only see an image of destruction sitting across from me.

"Branch—"

"So the pot… it must have been laced with something?"

"Yes. That's what we later figured out. It was mixed with some synthetic strands of cannabinoids that trigger abnormal activity in part of the brain."

I can't believe what I'm hearing. This kind of shit just

doesn't happen. But it *did* happen and we were all victims in one form or another. "And what about the child support? What did you do with it?"

Her gaze falls to her fingers twisting in her lap. "All of this was my doing. Had I been the supportive wife and been there for better or worse, none of this would've happened. But I was angry. Angry that I chose wrong. That I let go of my dreams to chase his. That I wasn't the kind of wife who could stand by her husband. And look at me now. I have nothing. No marriage. No degree. A brain that works when it wants. And love for a man who hates me the way I wanted him to."

"Tell me about the money, Mama," I say, ignoring her draw for sympathy and pressing for answers she's still reluctant to give.

"It's in the bank," she says, her voice sad, her eyes avoiding mine.

Something tightens in my abdomen. "What bank?"

"First National. In Iowa."

"All of it?"

"Yes," she says, finally looking up to meet my eyes.

There it is. That second punch in the gut I was waiting for. She's the cause of it all. "You let us suffer for nothing," I say, more to myself than to her.

She reaches out and places her hand over mine, but I instinctively recoil.

"We did all right, Branch. Didn't we?"

"If you call *all right* going without water, electricity, or food, then yeah, we sure as hell did all right. How could you do that to your own child? Do you have any idea how much I hated Dad for that? Or how many hours I put in at Jimmy's

Garage to help with bills? Not only did you keep me away from my father, you lied about him to make yourself look better."

"I'm sorry, Branch," she says, her eyes wet with tears. "I know an apology is never going to be enough. And I know I can't go back in time and do things differently, but if I could, I would. My head isn't screwed on right and it was even worse back then. I was constantly thinking Curtis was going to take you from me. At your age, you could have chosen which parent you wanted to live with, so I figured if you viewed him as an uncaring asshole, you'd always choose me."

She reaches out to me again, but I stand and place some distance between us. "Now is not the time. I don't want to be mean to you, so it'll do us both some good if you get out of my sight."

The hurt of her dismissal flashes across her face, mixing with the tears. "Okay… but promise me I haven't lost you." She rubs a hand over her wet cheeks. "Please. I couldn't bear if I lost you, Branch."

"Go, Mama. Just go."

I turn away from her and cast my gaze across the backyard. She robbed me of a father. She robbed my father of a son. I won't let her do that to Jace. Not anymore.

As for me, it may be too late. Growing up as I did placed something dark inside me that will always shy away from light.

Mama said we did *all right*. Truth is we *survived*! Thanks in part to food banks, second-hand stores and the kindness of friends. We barely scraped by. And now… to know that we suffered needlessly… I have no words.

A breeze fingers the wind chimes and stirs long-buried feelings.

I'm not a man of tears. Nor do I give into the weakness of emotions. They are pushed down. Repressed. Never to be acknowledged. But today, when a tear threatens, I let it fall. *Just that one.* I let it have its way, tracing a path along my jaw in mourning of what's lost and what will never be.

Chapter
SEVENTEEN

Branch

Present Day

"RAINE IS SCHEDULED TO MEET WITH US tomorrow afternoon, so I need you back in Dallas," Vaughn says. "Directly after we seal the deal—and we *will* seal the deal—there's a press conference to address the rumor mill. That's when we'll announce the Raine Industries endorsement and slide in our spin on your leave."

I press the speaker button and finish getting dressed. "Has something gone down that I need to know about?" I ask, detecting something strange in Vaughn's voice.

"Let's just say your absence from the last few practices hasn't gone unnoticed. Connie and I took care of it, but with you sitting out the next few games, we need your face on this one. We can't have anyone thinking you're stepping out for professional reasons. We need you in front of this."

"Yeah. Got it."

"We've already prepared your statement. Sending to you

within the hour. Look over it. Memorize it. Don't go off script. Too much is depending on getting this exactly right. We'll keep it short and sweet. And then at the right time, Connie will step in and end it."

"Got it," I repeat. "Thanks, V."

"I've gotta say, I'd enjoy this game far more if I were watching you play, Branch."

"I agree with Curtis. It's not the same when you aren't the one behind the ball," Jimmy says.

I take a swallow of beer. "Tell me about it." If someone would've told me—even a few hours ago—that I'd be sitting in Jimmy's man cave watching a playoff game with Jimmy and Dad, I would have dropped dead on the spot. And as for enjoying the game, I'm not. I've cursed the TV screen all four quarters, frustrated as hell that I'm here instead of on the field.

My phone dings. Recognizing the alert, I stop mid-conversation to check out the latest news. *ESPN* is reporting my leave—along with it, news of my endorsement with Raine Industries. I shake my head with a grin. *It's all playing out as Vaughn said it would.*

One less thing I have to worry about.

Dallas takes the win by a field goal. *A lucky one at that.* But at this point in the season, a win is a win.

"How's Mary taking all of this?" Dad asks as I walk him to his pickup. "Me and you, I mean."

"You know Mama. Head games and dramatics."

He chuckles. "Yeah, that's Mary all right. But otherwise, she's okay?"

I realize he's more concerned about Mama than he wants to let on. Does this mean he's… nah, can't be. "Yeah, she's in a good place. I think better than she's been in a while, but that's what scares the hell out of me. When she's doing well, she seems to think she's "cured" and goes off her meds. Then all hell breaks loose."

"But when she's herself, she's pretty amazing, isn't she?"

I lift a brow, giving Dad a sidelong glance. "Uh, yeah." *He can still say that about Mama? After all she's done? Hell, he must be crazier than she is.*

"I'd like to see her, Branch," he says casually.

"I don't think that's a good idea." Even though I'm pissed and have barely spoken to Mama since our *talk*, I struggle with the need to protect her. It's been this way for so long that it's become my default. It's always the same. She does something totally fucked up, yet I don't allow my anger to take over because I need to shield her. "You seem to be one of her triggers."

"Yeah, because she was afraid of the truth coming out. Now that everything's on the table, I think she'll be okay with my visit."

"Yeah, it's definitely all out there. I still can't believe any of it."

"Are you gonna be all right? With Mary? I know it's difficult learning the person you've championed for so many years has let you down in such a major way."

I sigh and run a hand through my hair. "Not gonna lie. It's been tough. For a minute, I considered walking away altogether and hiring a full staff to take care of her."

"What changed your mind?"

"Jace."

"He's lucky to have you," Dad says, stopping a few feet in front of his truck. "He and I are going out on Lake Blue Ridge tomorrow. You should come."

"We'll see."

"As for everything else, including me, take your time and sort through it all. And if there's anything I can do or explain, I'm here."

I nod, at a loss for words at the paternal overture that's been absent in my life.

"You never said, how did you take it when Mary told you that she and I are still married?"

My eyes widen. "What?"

"She didn't tell you?"

"No. She didn't."

I lie in bed and frown at the ceiling. Stuck here. In Blue Ridge. Sorting through more than I expected. More than I can comprehend. The truth can be as catastrophic as the lie. And I'm still unsure how I feel about either end of the spectrum, so I go through the motions.

Only one thing is certain at this point—I won't let Jace know the severity of Mama's ways. Of the damage she's caused. His view of her somehow remains untarnished, and although she doesn't deserve it, I'll make sure it stays that way.

Taking care of someone else, only carving out little edges for myself. That's how it's always been. And every day I'm home, I'm slapped with that reminder. When I'm in Dallas, I can forget. But here, there's no escape. I catch it from all sides. Twenty-four hours a day.

I toss and turn, unable to find sleep. I'm pissed off. Frustrated. And it will only get worse without the game. Without something or *someone* to pour those frustrations into.

"Fuck this." I reach for my phone and dial Connie.

"Branch?" She answers on the third ring. "Is that you?"

"Who else is brave enough to risk your wrath by calling at four in the morning?"

"True," she replies and clears her throat. "What is it? Is something wrong? Is your mother okay?"

"That's still up in the air. I'm not calling about that."

"Okay. What then?"

"Remember that girl who slid past security at the last postgame party?"

"Oh God. Which one?"

"The one who was screaming she wanted to touch me. You know… the one who threw her panties. Her card was attached. Remember? I asked you to hold on to it."

"Oh, *her*," Connie replies, the disdain obvious in her voice. "The over-the-top redhead. I remember that one."

"Do you still have the card?"

"I have every item I've received from your list of harlots, Branch."

I laugh. "Can you get her to Georgia?"

"For what? On second thought, never mind."

"Just for a night."

"You woke me up for this? You should be focused on your family and getting back to work, not on whose thighs you can get between."

"If you had any idea what I'm dealing with, you would've already arranged a different chick every night that I'm here. Besides"—my lips spread into a grin—"who says I'm gonna get between the redhead's thighs? Maybe I plan to hit it from the back."

"If I hadn't already fallen victim to your lewd remarks, I'd be offended."

"See, that's why you're my favorite press agent."

"I'd better be your *only* press agent for years to come."

"You will be. So do your job."

"Arranging your booty calls is *not* part of my job description," she fires back.

"But you do it so well. Come on, C. I'll get you that new car you've been wanting."

"The sordid things you talk me into," she mumbles and lets out a sigh. "Fine. When do you want her there?"

"Tomorrow."

"I suppose this is the part where I say I'll take care of it."

"Yep. And remember…"

"I know, I know. One night and then get her out."

"You're the best, Connie. You know that, right?"

"Just make sure I get that car. In red. And I want it by the end of the week."

"Consider it done."

"Branch?"

"Yeah?"

"You're actually buying me a car just for making arrangements to get you laid?"

"Come on, C. You know me better than that."

"True. So what gives?"

"Happy Birthday." After all Connie has done for me over the years, she deserves far more than a car, but I figure this is a good start.

She's irritating me already and it's only been ten minutes. "Sugar, what's with all the questions?"

"Sorry. I'm just surprised… and nervous. I didn't think I'd hear from you," she says.

"You didn't," I reply, pulling a couple of condoms from my pocket and dropping them on the bedside table. "You heard from my press agent."

I pull off my shirt, toss it on the bed, and step toward the opposite side of the room.

She opens her mouth to speak but momentarily falls silent, her eyes drawn to my chest. "Still. It's like a dream come true."

I study the attractive redhead. "Is it? So you dream about me?"

"A one-on-one with Branch McGuire? Are you kidding

me? What woman wouldn't kill to be in my shoes right now? I have to keep pinching myself to make sure this is all real."

My gaze travels the length of her body, my lips spreading into a slow smile when I see exactly what I expect—her eagerness to please me. To give me anything I want. Like all the others. It's in the way her eyes fall to the tenting of my gym shorts, the way her teeth sink into her bottom lip, and the way her nipples press against the thin fabric of her dress. "And just so there aren't any misconceptions, you do know why I invited you here?"

She takes a seat in the chair across from me and crosses her legs. The hint of lust in her blue eyes answers before she does. "I know precisely why I'm here. I didn't throw my panties at you just for the hell of it."

I laugh at her candor. "What's your name again?"

"Tori," she says.

Simple enough. A name I can easily remember. And just as easily forget. "Do you know what I think, Tori?"

"What?"

"I think you should take off your clothes and come show me exactly what you dream about."

I assume the seat next to the bed, the reason that prompted my call to Connie already pushed to the back of my thoughts. Tori stands and fingers the zipper of her dress, easing it down, exposing her creamy white skin and a rack most chicks would die for. She turns away from me, stepping out of the dress and bending over, sliding the thin material of her thong over her curves and down her legs.

"Nice ass."

"I'd like to think so," she says, tossing her dress onto the chair behind her and facing me, her fingers unclasping her bra and revealing the tight pebbles at the peaks of her breasts.

I slide my hand into my gym shorts, freeing my erection, already hard as stone. "Do you think you can handle this?"

She sucks in a breath, her steps faltering when her eyes fall to my cock. "I'm gonna give it the old college try." She lifts her gaze to mine and her expression unmasks her submission.

I wink at her. "Something tells me you're gonna do much more than try."

"Your cock is fucking gorgeous," she says, her eyes focused on my shaft. She falls to her knees, and without hesitation, she takes me whole into her mouth.

"Impressive," I whisper as she slowly feeds every inch of my dick between her lips a second time.

She's at the root, her suction tight as she pulls to the tip and twists her hand around me as she goes down again.

"Mmm," she moans, flattening her tongue against the underside on the way up. "You taste amazing." She kisses the head, licks the tip, and then her lips wrap around my dick, leisurely fucking me with her mouth. And it feels fucking incredible. My hips lift, meeting her, urging her to take me all the way to the back of her throat. And she does.

Again.

Again.

And again.

She looks up. Her eyes hot on mine, moaning around my dick as she tastes me. I watch her tongue tracing the crown, her lips parting as they move over my shaft, and the lust in her gaze as she swallows me.

"Yeah, just like that," I murmur, my thighs clenching as I get harder.

She moves into her rhythm again, her mouth drawing up and down over the thick length of my cock. I close my eyes and recline my head, taking pleasure in the warm wet of her mouth as it envelopes my dick with each full stroke. Her movement is slow and purposeful, and although it feels good as fuck, I want better than *good*. I deserve her best effort, and if she doesn't know how to give it, I'll take pleasure in showing her.

I sift my fingers through her hair and grip a handful, standing and moving her with me. Only then do I take control of her, plunging and driving into her mouth with fierce repetition.

"That's better," I grunt, picking up the pace, fucking her mouth with an aggressive rapidity that hits the back of her throat with each thrust. Her lips tighten around me, and her eyes water as I plow deeper into her mouth.

She gasps for air, struggling to keep up, her hands gripping the back of my thighs for leverage.

My balls tighten. The crown of my cock prickles and my release comes barreling to the surface. And then, gripping both sides of her head, I climax with a long groan.

I look down at her, our eyes making contact. "I want you to swallow it. All of it."

She nods her compliance and I flood her mouth, spurting in long waves until my come is slipping along the edge of her lips.

When she's licked me clean, I motion for her to stand and I lift her, carrying her to the king-size bed and placing her directly in front of me. Grabbing the black packet from the bedside table, I rip the foil, pull out the condom, and roll it over my length.

Tori props on her elbows, her legs spread, her breathing shallow, and her eyes crawling over me.

I grasp her ankles and pull her to the edge of the bed. My hands move under her thighs, pushing her legs back until her feet are over her head. Within the next second, I'm driving into her with a deep thrust.

"Oh fuuuck," she cries out.

I bring my eyes to hers. "You good?"

"Yes," she gasps. "Don't stop."

With a firm grip on her thighs, I pull out. And on my next plunge into her hot channel, I move deeper, the head of my cock hitting the end of her.

"Oh my God. Oh my God. Oh my God." The words slip from her lips with each rock of my pelvis.

In and out.

Over.

Over.

And over.

Relentlessly, I pummel into her wet center as her moans fill the room. And that's all I want to hear. Not the questions I don't intend to answer. Not the fascination she has with me. I didn't have Connie arrange her visit for that... didn't have her fly first class for that. And I didn't put her up in the best hotel Blue Ridge has to offer for that.

All I want is *this*. Her pussy. Her beneath me. Her legs spread and my cock planted inside her, working her over and taking from her what I need. Fucking her until she's breathless, until she's gasping my name in tandem with that final stroke, and then I want to send her back to wherever she came from.

I look into her eyes and tell her how wet her pussy is.

How hot it is. How it feels better with each stroke. I say all the dirty little words that make the walls of her sex pulse. And I whisper the shameful taunts that make her clench tighter around me. I watch as the ferocity of my thrusts plays out in her expressions. She wants more. She can take more, so I take the liberty of giving it. I make damn sure her trip is worth it, giving her tight little cunt a fucking it won't soon forget, hitting those spots that make her moans deeper, her cries louder, and her pussy wetter. Yeah, I'm pretty fucking sure she'll never forget this night.

But despite what this redhead said, I know this can't be what any woman dreams about. Being treated this way. Being nothing more than a vessel for my frustrations. And that's all she is. Someone to pour my load into. Someone whose name I'll forget as soon as the door closes behind her. Yeah, I'm a raging asshole, but at least I'm honest about it.

Chapter
EIGHTEEN

Ragan

Present Day

OVERHEARING HAYLEY ON THE PHONE, I stare at her—incredulous—as she arranges a sitter for her cat Channing Tatum.

"Sorry about that," she says when she ends the call. "Mom and Dad won't help out, so I had to make other arrangements. Can you believe them?"

"Er… what do you mean?"

"Mom expects me to leave Channing Tatum at home for five hours by himself while she parties with her 'lady friends,'" she air quotes. "And Dad, he's practically useless." She rolls her eyes and takes a sip of her iced tea. "Now that Channing Tatum is sick, Dad treats him like he's a burden."

"I'm sorry." That's about all I can muster. I can't relate to her affection for the feline version of Channing Tatum. If she had the real thing, well, that would be an entirely different story.

"Thanks for not saying anything weird like you usually do."

Me weird? You're the one throwing away good money on a sitter for a cat you call Channing Tatum. Of all the names you could have chosen, you give that crazy cat the name of one of the sexiest guys on the planet. I'd love to see your Channing Tatum pull off a Magic Mike lap dance that brings in nearly two hundred million at the box office. Yeah, I'm the weird one. Of course, I don't say any of this aloud because she appears so torn up about the state of her beloved pet. "Are you gonna be okay?" I ask.

"Yeah. But I've gotta go. I have to pick up Channing Tatum's prescription and get him to the sitter's. I'll call you later and you can fill me in on Mr. Celebrity," she teases, looking over her shoulder at Branch and back at me, fanning herself with her hands. "He's so flippin' hot!"

"Speaking of *Mr. Celebrity,* I need to get his order in. And I stand by what I said last night—cut your losses with that lowlife boyfriend. You deserve better."

We hug goodbye and she walks across the dining area toward the exit. I stare after Hayley and wonder how the hell she's gonna cope with a broken heart *and* the loss of Channing Tatum.

Regardless of the impending heartache, she needs to dump that cheating ass Derick. I should've done the same when Ethan cheated on me. I saw the signs, but like Hayley, I was quick to assume it was something else. I'd *wanted* it to be something else. I'd initially attributed the changes I'd seen in Ethan to his new work schedule. But even after he'd had time to adjust to the night shift, he remained distant. So my next assumption was that he was internalizing the pressures of fatherhood. His dad was an abusive, alcoholic deadbeat, so Ethan was determined to do better by our daughter. But when that assumption went south, I latched on to the next possibility. To be honest, I'd thought up countless excuses. And although the proof had been staring me right in the face, I'd chosen to ignore it.

Ethan stopped touching me like he used to. His deep passionate kisses all but disappeared. And the desperation he'd always held for my body became a thing of the past. I knew what all the signs pointed to, but instead of addressing the obvious, I endeavored to spice up our sex life. Raunchy fishnet outfits, expensive sex toys, and extremely naughty sexts. Doing whatever he asked of me in bed and out. I was willing to give any and everything to keep my family intact. And to my heart's content, my efforts pulled him back in. But a short while later, I found myself again vying for his attention. I refused to acknowledge he was cheating... until undisputable evidence fell into my lap.

I was devastated, embarrassed, heartbroken. But at the same time, I didn't want to leave him. I wanted my family. He knew that was my weakness, and he played it to his advantage, saying he wanted the same, swearing he'd never cheat again, then wooing me like he'd done in the beginning. He promised to regain my trust and begged for my forgiveness. And stupidly enough, I gave it, only to have it all blow up in my face again. Two months later, I left. Sadly it wasn't because of the cheating; it was for something far worse.

I won't sit back and watch Hayley degrade herself as I did. I simply won't.

Branch has become somewhat of a regular patron at the diner. He always comes alone, always around the same time, and always sits at the same table. A lot of sameness, but he's different somehow. Yes, when he isn't looking, I ogle. So I notice the differences. Probably more than I should, but it's difficult not to. He's hot as fuck. Totally dream worthy and always pulling an instant purr from kitty. But lately, he's less playful, somewhat pensive. Truth be told, he's less asshatish. So we only exchange one or two jabs instead of our typical nine or ten. Guess whatever crawled up his ass has finally crawled out.

So to my dismay, there isn't anything to fill Hayley in on regarding *Mr. Celebrity*. He comes in, places his order, signs a few autographs, eats his food, then leaves. And either I'm finally getting this waitress thing down, or my luck is starting to change. I've made no mistakes with his orders. But that probably has more to do with the fact that he always orders the same flavorless meal than it does my waitressing skills. And his tips… well, they still sit on the short side in my opinion. His orders total a little over seven bucks. He always pays with a ten and says, "Keep the change."

It's Wednesday, the only day Jim Bob's Diner closes early. And as I approach the end of my shift, Branch breezes in for the second time, looking for something he thinks he may have dropped during lunch. After a quick search, he heads back out, my eyes focused on his backside until the door closes behind him.

Jim Bob and I are the only two left in the diner. He's in the back locking up and I'm up front going through my closing routine. There isn't a lot to do considering how much Carrie took care of before she left. So thankfully, I finish earlier than I normally would. After flipping off the jukebox, I head to the locker for my purse. I sling the strap across my body and head back to the front, relieved to see my boss already waiting near the exit.

I head to my Jeep Liberty as Jim Bob locks the door and sets the alarm. Other than my car and Jim Bob's, one other vehicle is in the parking lot—a red convertible. And someone is bent over the back seat, I'd guess looking for something. And since I had a good view a short while ago, I easily identify that taut ass. He's probably still looking for whatever he lost.

"Have a good evening, Ragan," Jim Bob says, interrupting my thoughts when he catches up to me.

"You, too. See you in the morning," I reply and scramble into my car. "Another day, another corn on my foot." I kick off my shoes and after buckling in, I insert the key into the ignition and turn it forward, but the car doesn't crank. I try again. Same thing. I flip on the lights. They work. I try the horn. It works, too. Now what?

I glance in the rearview mirror and see Jim Bob pulling out of the lot, and then a couple of parking spaces to the right, up pops the head of the person who was leaning over the back seat of the convertible. And yup, it's definitely Branch. His eyes catch mine. I quickly look away and try to start the car again, but get the same result.

"Just great," I mumble and grab my phone. I dial Hayley, but it goes to voicemail. I next try Aunt Sophie, and when she doesn't answer, I remember she's at Bible class, so I hang up. With Dad and Uncle Stan on the road, who else can I call? No way will I call Jim Bob back. And Carrie is at bingo with her mama. There's Patty. I suppose I could call her. But after considering my living situation, I decide I don't want to explain yet another broken-home story, so I try Hayley again. By the second ring, there's a tap on my door. I end the call, turn the ignition enough to give power to the control panel, and lower the window.

"Need some help?" Branch asks.

"Nope."

"You sure? I can take a look. It could be an easy fix."

I almost ask what he can possibly know about repairing cars until I remember he worked in a garage throughout high school. "Okay, sure. Have at it."

He walks around to the front of the car, lifts the hood, and after a quick inspection, he tells me to give it a try. I turn the switch and hear a clicking noise. And then nothing. He tinkers with something for a minute or two and then asks me to try it again. I twist the key in the ignition, and just when it sounds as if the car is going to crank, it goes silent. After Branch does his tinkering thing again, I cross my fingers and pray that whatever he did works this time. But when I rotate the switch, there's no sound at all. Not even the click.

Branch steps to the side of the car and says, "I think your starter's gone."

"Crap. I was afraid of that."

"So you were aware of the problem and did nothing about it?" he asks, his tone reproving.

"A friend of my ex kinda worked on it, but it was a temporary fix."

Branch lowers the hood. "So that means you're gonna need a ride."

I lift my phone, waving it at him. "Yep, I'll call a friend."

"The same *friend* you've already called and who's not picking up?"

I lower the phone as I consider trying Hayley again. But if she's on her date, the likelihood of her answering is slight.

"It'll be dark pretty soon and you shouldn't be out here alone. I can give you a ride. It's no problem. Come on."

He opens my door, and reluctantly, I step out of the car and follow him. My heart rate spikes a beat faster with each step. And my eyes are stuck to his backside. He truly is something to look at. Tall, broad shouldered, muscular, and with a face that puts even the top male models to shame. In high school, we called him a *pretty boy*. Over the years, he's gotten even prettier. And the way he moves—visibly arrogant, with an athletic grace—oh fuck me. He's *beyond* irresistible. Yes, I can say it to myself, but I won't tell him even though I'm positive he already knows it.

I give Branch my address and he plugs it into his phone's GPS. And then the ride to my place is ten kinds of awkward. He asks how long I've been working at Jim Bob's. And then he asks if I'll be working tomorrow. I tell him I have the morning shift. Then he offers to pick me up and without thinking, I accept. And that's it. The remainder of the ride is a shroud of silence. But internally, Miss Kitty is purring, prowling, and clawing at my lady bits. When I finally manage to suppress my urges, I consider this scenario. I'm riding in a car with Branch Fucking McGuire. I don't want it to seem like a big deal, but it kinda sorta is.

When he pulls into my drive, we sit for a moment, neither

of us saying a thing, until I blurt out, "Hey, I can get a ride in the morning, so no need to pop up." I grab the door handle and add, "Thanks for getting me home."

Branch's phone rings right as I open the door and reach for my shoes. Before I get one foot out of the car, he leans over and grasps my wrist asking me to wait. After telling the caller they're all set for tomorrow, he explains that he's catching up with a friend and then ends the call.

Friend? I'm not his friend.

He sits back, coolly draping his arm over the seat. "Why the rush?"

For several long seconds, I stare at him like a deer in headlights. I part my lips and remind myself to speak, but the words catch in my throat. I meet his eyes and search his face. *He knows.* He's perfectly aware of his power to leave women speechless. *Say something.* "Um… you gave me a ride home. And we're here, so this is the part where I say thanks and get out."

His brow arches. "Oh, is that how it works?"

I give him a nervous smile. *Oh geez. Why am I nervous?* Because I don't have the diner and its patrons as a buffer, that's why. "Yes, pretty much. Unless you're waiting for me to give you gas money. Judging by your tips, you're obviously a little short on cash these days."

He throws his head back with a deep throaty laugh. "You seem to have a comeback for just about everything."

"Do I? I haven't noticed."

"So how would it work if I were to ask you out? Would you have a comeback for that?"

Is he fucking with me again?

"Ah, so no smartass remark for that one, huh? Let me help

you out. I'm asking. And you respond by saying yes."

I *should* respond by getting out of this car, yet I remain in place. I don't want to say no to him, but I'm not so stupid as to say yes either. My insides are a mess of knots. "Er… I don't think so."

"Wait." He grabs my wrist again when I turn to get out. "Why would you say no?"

I'm not crazy and I'm very much aware of the way my sex clenches at the mere thought of Branch McGuire. And I've already imagined lying skin to skin underneath him as he does unimaginable things to kitty, but that's just it—I know it's all in my head. He's trying to stroke his ego. To satisfy the part of himself that's never had a woman deny him, especially a woman like me. I know it's a game. And today is no different than it was in high school. I'm not pretty enough, I'm not thin enough, and I'm not good enough for someone like him to do anything more than what he's doing right now—toying with me. "Why would I say yes?"

His eyebrows scrunch. "Is that a serious question?"

"I asked, didn't I?"

"Because I'm Branch McGuire. Women don't tell me no."

"Apparently they do," I say and hop out of the car.

He calls after me, but I don't break my stride and I don't look back. I walk up the drive and before I get to the front door, it swings open and an excited Cecelia runs out to me. Picking up my baby girl, I spin her around, instantly lost in her giggles. A few moments later, I hear Branch pulling away.

I place Branch's check on the table. "Why do you bother coming here for lunch? This street is lined with restaurants that suit your kind a lot better than this place."

"Does your boss know you're suggesting his customers dine elsewhere?" he asks and shoves the remainder of the bunless turkey burger into his mouth.

"It's not like you're getting a five-star meal," I say, ignoring his question. "Isn't that more of what you're accustomed to?"

He gives me a wink. "Maybe I like the scenery here."

My cheeks warm and I think back to the question he asked last night. "Even if you're serious, you're wasting your time." He gives me a strange look, and I almost think he recognizes me, so I ask, "You don't remember me, do you?"

"From?"

"Figures."

"No. Tell me," he says. "Then I can kick myself for forgetting."

"It's no biggie. You probably forget most of the people you meet."

"Are you saying I'd forget you? Because I don't think so."

You already have. "If you don't want anything else, I need to get to my other tables. I've not been on the receiving end of the boss's tongue lashings lately and I want to keep it that way," I say, looking over my shoulder for Jim Bob.

Branch ignores my plea and proceeds with his own agenda. "Let's say I came back to ask you out... again. Are you telling me you'd say no?"

"If you want your ego bruised, ask me and find out."

"So, you'd actually say no? To *me*?" Disbelief colors his tone.

"Well, at least I know who your biggest fan is. And it's

obvious you think you can breeze in here, flex your muscles, bat those girly eyelashes, and I'll fawn all over you. But if I were you, I wouldn't hold my breath."

"So you've noticed these guns?" he asks, flexing and admiring his biceps.

I roll my eyes and shake my head. "How could I not? You walk into the diner wearing a skintight compression shirt. And you know very well the impact that will have on *any* woman with a pulse. I mean, I know you guys wear those when you play ball or work out, but just to walk around in? Real douchebag move."

"So now I'm a douchebag?" he asks, his eyes locked onto mine. There's humor in his baby blues, but I fail to see the joke.

"I didn't say *you* were a douchebag. I said guys who wear those tight workout shirts are."

"Same difference."

"Whatever. Would you like anything else?" I ask, passing him the dessert menu, knowing he never orders dessert.

"So, you honestly expect me to believe you're not interested in me?"

"I don't know how many ways I can tell you. You're seriously barking up the wrong tree."

His brows rise, an expression of understanding crossing his handsome face. "Oh, so you're into chicks?"

My mouth falls open.

"No big deal if you have a girlfriend. She can come along." He leans toward me, grabbing the hem of my skirt, his eyes hot on mine. "Sugar, I assure you that each of those cunts will get a proper fucking."

My eyes widen and I swallow dry air. Then I try to

respond, but my voice has suddenly taken leave.

He tips his head, gesturing toward kitty. "Unless that little thing is greedy and you don't want to share. Is that it? Do you want me all to yourself?"

"Oh. My. God." I can't believe the balls on this guy but holy shit am I ever turned on... actually more than turned on. *But how could I not be? It's Branch Freaking McGuire!* And this... *him*... the way he's looking at me, the indecent little words slipping from his sinfully perfect lips, it's like waving an insanely large bag of catnip in front of a real kitty. And if he only knew how greedy my *little thing* could be, how tightly it would squeeze every inch of his cock, he'd take me right here. And I'd let him. Oh, how I'd let him. *Fuck.* What am I doing? *This is Branch fucking with me... again.* I jerk my skirt from his grasp and take a few paces back. "I'm so done here."

"Hold up. Wait." He grins. "Forget I said that. I'm just fuckin' around. I'd like to get a coffee to go."

After a long beat and a brief recovery, I ask, "How would you like it?"

"Black."

"Finally." I snatch the menu out of his hand and he laughs as I step to my next table. After jotting down the orders of the other customers in my station, I walk the slips back to the kitchen and pin them to the cook's carrousel.

When I step back out to the main dining area, I find Branch has moved to the counter.

"A family came in and needed a larger table, so I gave them mine," he explains and continues flipping through what I quickly recognize as my sketch pad.

"I didn't know you could draw."

I snatch the pad and place it under the counter. "And I didn't know you were clueless as to the concept of personal property."

He shrugs at my reproof. "I was just appreciating your work. You're good. *Really* good."

"Thanks." I place the coffee in front of him.

"What else do you draw?" he asks, his piercing blue eyes intent on mine.

My cheeks heat. I never discuss my art. *With anyone*. Each drawing is a deeply personal representation of me. "Random stuff. Emotions. Abstract things."

"Nothing figurative?"

"Not really."

"Why?" he asks.

"I just don't."

"I think you should." He grabs his coffee and slides from the stool with a smirk. "And if you change your mind about that threesome, let me know."

Chapter
NINETEEN

Ragan

TAKING A BREAK FROM THE 1950s, I STEP OUTSIDE the diner for a breath of fresh air. Not even a foot from the door, I notice a truck in the place where my car should be. *What the hell?*

My steps quicken as I make my way to the parking lot, but I come to an abrupt halt when I discover what's happening. A red tow truck with *Jimmy's Garage* imprinted on the side is in my spot. And behind it, is my car, hooked to a pulley as Branch guides it toward the flatbed.

"What do you think you're doing?" I ask when I reach him.

He glances over his shoulder at me and turns back to the controls on the tow. "I figured you'd need your car, so getting it fixed is probably in your best interest."

"So you're my self-appointed fairy godfather now? Thanks, but no thanks. I don't need your help. I manage just fine on my own."

Branch continues with the lift as if I didn't offer the slight-est of objections. I walk around to face him, momentarily thrown off by the change in his appearance. He's dressed differently today—wearing a Redhorns cap flipped to the back, a snug-fitting black T-shirt, and ripped jeans. And he looks a little dirty. As if he's been working on cars all morning, giving him the look of a greasy mechanic. But not the sleazy kind who'll overcharge you and then promise a discount if you let him feel you up. Branch is the hot, sexy kind. The kind you hope bends you over the hood of a car and gives your pussy the tune-up you didn't know it needed.

"Did you hear what I said? I don't need your help."

He lifts his gaze to mine. "Who says I'm doing it for you?"

"It's *my* car, so who are you doing it for if not me?" I ask, my hand going to my hip.

"You have a kid, right?"

"Yeah," I reply, wondering what CeeCee has to do with this. "How did you know?"

Branch flips the switch on the side of the flatbed and the Jeep starts its slow crawl onto the back of the truck. "The other day, when I gave you a ride home. A little girl came running out to you. I figured she was yours."

"Yes, that was my daughter."

When the car comes to a stop, he removes his gloves and shoves them into his back pocket. "Let's just say I'm doing it for her."

Now *that*, I didn't expect. Not that I expected *any* of this. "Again, I'm asking why."

We share a fleeting glance as he steps past me and shuts off the control switch inside the truck. "I know how it is to be short on cash but to still have a responsibility to your family. Kids shouldn't suffer on account of poor parental decisions."

"Excuse me?" I go from surprised to offended in the

measure of a second.

"Hey, you about ready, Branch?"

I look behind the irresistibly hot ball player and see a handsome, dark-haired man approaching us. He's older—I'd say midfifties. His gray polo shirt reads *Jimmy's Garage* and he's wearing a friendly smile and holding two cups of coffee.

"One of those is mine, right?" Branch asks.

"Not unless you're paying," he replies, grinning as he passes a cup to Branch. "I'm Jimmy." He extends his hand. "You must be Ragan."

"Yes, I am. And if you're waiting on this one to pay for anything"—I tip my head toward Branch—"you're gonna have a long wait."

Jimmy's brows lift in surprise. "Really? I've known Branch to be quite generous."

"Well, speaking as a waitress, I can't say the same."

"You're using the term *waitress* pretty loosely, don't you think?" Branch asks.

"Hey, your orders have been completely error free."

"And we both know that's been sheer luck. I'm actually worried about what I'll get if I order anything different," he replies, his eyes on me, his expression stoic.

"Obviously, you aren't too worried because you keep coming back to *my* station."

"Do I need to give you guys a minute?" Jimmy asks, his eyebrows shooting together in confusion.

"Nope." Branch keeps his eyes on mine. "This one's scared of me."

"He's harmless, Ragan," Jimmy says. "Don't let his aggressive ladies' man act fool you."

I break eye contact with Branch and turn to Jimmy, who

gives me a kind smile. I sense he's the type of man who always wears a smile, and I instantly take a liking to him.

"Not to worry. None of his acts fool me," I reply and redirect my attention to Branch. "I know exactly what kind of person he is."

Branch spins his cap to the front, lowers the brim, then casually leans against Jimmy's truck. "Yeah, and what kind is that?"

"I think we both know what kind, *sugar.*"

Branch chuckles at my use of his pet name.

Jimmy starts to say something but stops. He squints at Branch and his expression shifts as though something suddenly occurs to him. "You must have made a real impression on Branch," he says, as his gaze flashes back to me, his lips curved into an odd smile. "He called last night saying he needed to get your car to my garage first thing. And just to be sure I followed through, he was waiting on me this morning when I arrived."

My eyes track back over to Branch as he brings the coffee to his lips. "What?" he asks in response to the question I didn't voice aloud.

I turn back to Jimmy. "It's the starter. I'm not sure if it can be patched up until I get enough money to get a new one. It takes awhile for it to turn over sometimes, and yesterday it wouldn't do anything."

"Don't worry about it," Jimmy says. "We'll check it out and have it fixed up for you in no time."

"I may not be able to pay for all of this right away," I say, embarrassed at the state of my finances.

"I'll take care of it," Branch offers. "Whatever the cost I'll—"

"No, I pay my own way." My tone is stern, making it clear I don't intend to accept any additional handouts from him.

"Just trying to help, but I forgot, you don't need any help. You manage just fine on your own," he mimics. He places his cup on the seat of the truck, then steps to the flatbed, strapping my tires and securing the chains.

"Branch says you have a little girl."

"I do," I reply and wonder what else Branch has told Jimmy about me. Did he tell him he's offered up a threesome? *A scenario that got me off three times last night.*

"I have four," Jimmy says.

"Wow! Four girls."

"I know. I still find it surprising each time I say it aloud. And my wife is seven months along with our fifth."

"Congratulations," I say, wondering how anyone can manage five kids. I often struggle with my one.

"Thanks."

"You must *really* love kids," I tell him.

"I do," he says with a laugh. "Hey, I have an idea that may solve your car-repair issue."

"I'm all ears."

"We're having dinner tonight at my place. Somewhat of a celebration for Branch, his kid brother, and his dad. My wife Loretta gets tired pretty easy these days, and I try to help out as much as she allows, but she's a little on the stubborn side. Tries to do everything the way she did before the pregnancy, but at seven months, she needs to slow it down. Which is where you come in."

"I don't think I follow," I reply, still confused.

"Come over for dinner. You and your daughter. She'll have a great time with my girls, and in the meantime, if you can convince Loretta to let you help with the meal, I'll knock half off the cost of your repair."

I glance over at Branch for clarification, but he shrugs, so I look back at Jimmy. "That's kind of strange, don't you think? You don't even know me."

"But Branch does, and you'd *really* be helping me out. Loretta insists on doing things on her own. And I can see you're much the same." Worry lines crease his forehead. "I love my wife's independent spirit, but I know she's overdoing it. So, if you offer to help her and then refuse to accept *no* for an answer..."

The concern in his brown eyes squeezes my heart. I instinctively want to help him. "If I wear her down, you can avoid another argument about your helping out and about her doing too much."

"Exactly. So this kills two birds. And besides, if you're a friend of his"—he gestures toward Branch—"then you're a friend of mine. And well, friends help friends."

Branch steps to the front of the truck and grabs his coffee. "No, she isn't my friend. She's afraid to be my friend." He chuckles and takes a sip.

"I didn't think you had female friends," I shoot at him.

"I don't," Branch replies.

"Then I fail to see the issue here." I stare at him until Jimmy breaks the silence.

"What time does your shift end?" Jimmy asks.

"Two."

"Perfect. Branch can pick you up. He'll get you home to change and get your daughter. And you can be at our place at five."

"Um... okay," I say, not knowing what I've agreed to.

"Nice meeting you, Ragan," Jimmy says, smiling at me like the cat who ate the canary.

"You, too," I reply, wondering what's behind the strange smile.

He makes his way to the truck, leaving me standing face-to-face with Branch, whose gaze is so heated, I swear it burns right through my clothes. "Why are you looking at me like that?"

"Like what?"

"Like, you're... like I'm... as though you can..."

"What? Do you feel naked when I look at you?" His voice is low and seductive as he steps closer, surrounding me with nothing but him. "That's okay, you don't have to answer." His gaze drops to my blouse. "I know you do. Maybe you should tell your employer to invest in shirts that don't reveal the nipples of his employee's tits. Not that I'm complaining."

I swear the peaks of my breasts get even tighter. I cross my arms over my chest to hide the evidence of my arousal. "I don't know what you're up to, but whatever you're doing, stop."

"Just so we're clear, what is it that I should stop doing? Eating at the diner? Giving a stranded woman a ride home? Helping someone with a car repair?"

"All of it," I say, looking him directly in the eyes. "Stop all of it and mind your own business."

"You heard Jimmy. We're all friends here," he says. "And friends help friends." He glances over his shoulder at Jimmy, who's sitting in the truck on the phone, and turns back to me. "And if you stop being so weird, I'll help you with the one thing I know you *really* want." He winks at me and follows it up. "I'll see you at two, sugar."

Ugh. *Oh God. Why does my heart sound like it's stumbling to find the correct beat?* I hate how he gets to me. And why hasn't he stopped calling me sugar?

I stand in the parking lot watching them haul off my Jeep Liberty and thinking that even though I'd refused to go out with him, I still somehow have a date with Branch McGuire.

Chapter
TWENTY

Ragan

WHY DID I AGREE TO JIMMY'S OFFER? AND WHY did I let Branch and him haul off my car? Was the whole rescue-and-repair scenario a ploy? I can't imagine Branch going that far to land a date with someone like me. Or with any woman for that matter. Besides, Jimmy doesn't seem the type to play those games. And Branch surely doesn't need a wingman to secure time with women. So, what gives?

I rewind it all in my head, and the only thing I'm sure of is that Branch seems to run hot and cold. A condescending asshat half the time, and then today and the day before, he's nice to me. He *went out of his way* to be nice to me.

Over the years, I've read and heard many things about Branch McGuire, most of which was about his stats and playboy lifestyle. Never have I heard anything about his kindness. Sure, he donates to charities and attends fundraising events. What professional athlete doesn't? But random acts of kindness? I figure those are as rare for him to *give* as they are for me to *receive.*

Yet here I am, on the receiving end of it. And now I'm riddled with guilt. I was so busy being snarky and suspicious, that I failed to show my appreciation. Little does Branch know how much I owe him. Not only is he helping me out of a situation I couldn't find a way to resolve, he's sparing me the humiliation of asking Dad or Aunt Sophie to borrow their cars or even worse—to drive me around like a kid.

But maybe that would have been easier to swallow than what I'm facing tonight. Not that I have any reason to be, but part of me is nervous about this dinner. The only thing keeping me from freaking out is that it's not an *actual* date. It's a means to an end, a way to pay for my car repair. I guess I could call it *work*.

Then again, I *am* having dinner at a certain time, at a certain place, and with a certain someone, and by definition, that's a *date,* right? Holy hell, I don't know. Whatever it is, the mere thought of being close to Branch gives me butterflies.

And that isn't good.

Branch is standing beside the red convertible, arms crossed, leaning on the driver's door when I step out of the diner. I'm not sure why, but I figured he'd be late. And ten minutes ago, when Carrie told me he was outside waiting, my stomach did one heck of a somersault.

Carrie was as excited as I was nervous when I filled her in on the last few days. Of course she thought I was missing half my marbles for declining Branch's initial date invitation. And then she thought I'd lost the other half for not offering to take him behind Jim Bob's and showing him—in the flesh— exactly how hard my nipples were.

She also gave me some last-minute advice, which I had no intention of taking. I mean, seriously, if I did even half of what she suggested, I'd end up in the county lockup. But I listened anyway, the whole time second-guessing my decision to help Jimmy but knowing it's what I need to do if I want to settle my bill.

As usual, Branch looks all kinds of hot, in jeans that hang low where his waist narrows, a button-down shirt left open and a sky-blue fitted T-shirt underneath. Hmm. No compression shirt? That's twice now. Wonder if that has anything to do with my douchebag comments or if it's just a coincidence.

When I'm only a few feet away, his eyes grab mine and then he says, "Hey."

That's it. Just *hey* and I swear, it's the sexiest thing I've ever heard in my life. I scoff at my earlier thought—no way will this smokin' hotness *ever* need a wingman. He can melt the panties off any woman who's lucky enough to stand in his line of vision. I should know because mine just went *poof*.

"Hey," I repeat as I come to a stop a few feet in front of the car. Self-conscious, I don't move, my eyes locking on his, and I wonder what he's thinking when he looks at me. Is he picturing me naked, or do I just feel that way?

"Ragan, have a great evening with Branch and Jimmy," comes a loud voice from behind me.

I turn toward the diner and see my coworker standing in the doorway, waving and smiling from ear to ear.

Way to go, Carrie. Now Branch knows he's been the topic of conversation. I'm sure he just loves that.

"How's it going, Branch?" Carrie asks, still managing to sound sexy even with her outside voice.

He lifts his chin.

"Be sure to show my friend a good time," she says. "And by 'good time,' I mean the horizontal kind. Ragan is way overdue."

Branch actually grins at Carrie's craziness while I fight the urge to turn and walk in the opposite direction. *I'm going to kill her!*

"Goodbye, Carrie," I say, glancing over my shoulder, hoping to shut her up and push her back into the diner.

My eyes return to the guy who's making my stomach queasy. He tips his head, motioning toward the opposite side of the car. I take his cue as he walks around the rear, meeting me and opening my door. As I slide inside the car, I exhale a puff of anxiety and remind myself to play it cool.

"How was work?" Branch asks when he's seated next to me, closing his door and bringing his fresh soap-musk scent to my nose. Mmm. He smells yummy.

"Work was work. And surprise, surprise. I didn't get any of my orders wrong," I reply, already on the defensive.

With a shake of his head, he cranks the car. "So, I see a normal conversation with you is out of the question."

Ugh. *Why do I always go into bitchy defense mode with him*? I decide to append my reply with a non-bitch response, but before I get one word out, Branch flips on the radio and increases the volume, effectively muting the possibility of a *normal* conversation.

Chapter
TWENTY-ONE

Branch

"THIS MUST BE YOUR DAUGHTER."

"Yes," Ragan replies with a smile that beams of pride and affection for her child.

I crouch in front of the little brown-eyed girl who's the spitting image of her mother. "Hi. My name is Branch."

Her forehead furrows as if she's deep in thought, then her eyes widen. "Like on a tree?"

I grin at her. "Yes, like on a tree."

She flashes her tiny white teeth. "That's silly."

I consider her words and respond, "Yes, I suppose it is. So what's your name?"

She looks up at Ragan as if asking if it's okay to talk to this stranger. Ragan gives her a nod, and the little girl looks back to me. "Cecelia," she says in a low voice.

I give her a smile of encouragement. "That's a pretty name for a very pretty girl."

She slides a finger in her mouth as her lips curl upward.

"What do you say, CeeCee?" Ragan asks.

Still casting her timid smile, she twists her fingers in her hair. "Thank you."

"How old are you, Cecelia?" I ask.

She lifts two fingers, and using her other hand, she forces a third finger into the holdup.

"You're a big girl, huh?"

She grins and nods.

"Do you know what I've heard?" I ask.

She shakes her head at me.

"I've heard that three-year-old girls named Cecelia love strawberry ice cream with sprinkles on top. Is that true?"

"Yes," she replies, louder than anything she's said up till now.

"Would you like some?"

"Yes."

I look up at Ragan. "What do you say, Mom? Can we take the prettiest little girl in Blue Ridge out for strawberry ice cream with sprinkles?"

Ragan grasps her daughter's hand. "Come here, sweetie. I need to talk to Branch for a second, so can you go to our room and pick out a coloring book for us?"

"Okay, Mommy," she replies and looks back at me. "Don't leave, Branch." She scampers off.

When Cecelia is out of earshot, Ragan turns to me, her expression the exact opposite of what I expect. "Look, I don't know what kind of game you're playing, but don't bring my daughter into it."

"Are you always so damned paranoid? Why must it be a game? Why can't it be a guy doing something nice for a little girl?"

"Why?" She crosses her arms over her chest. "Surely there's a reason."

"Yeah, there is," I reply, getting fed up with her attitude. "Her mom is tired and her dad is an asshole who's probably not doing his part. If he were, he'd make sure the mother of his child is taken care of. Which means he would've been the one you called when you were stranded after work, and he's also the one who'd be helping with the car repair. So I'm guessing he's absent most of the time. And maybe, just maybe, I know how that can be for a kid."

Ragan shuts down her accusatory gaze and her defensive stance relaxes. "I'm sorry," she says, on an exhale. "People rarely do things without looking for something in return and you've been—"

"I've been what?"

"You've been kinder at times than what I've come to expect, and I don't quite know how to take it."

"Well, how about this? Don't take it *any* way. Accept that someone's being nice."

"Okay, I think I can do that."

"Good. My brother is waiting in the car. The ice cream parlor is kinda one of our hangouts when I'm in town. We aren't due at Jimmy's until five and we have about forty-five minutes to spare, so are you in?"

"I can't disappoint the prettiest little girl in Blue Ridge, now can I?"

Ragan calls for Cecelia and she comes rushing into the room, screaming for strawberry ice cream.

"See what you've started," Ragan says.

CeeCee gives her backpack to Ragan and rushes over to me. I pick her up and ask what size ice cream she wants. As we narrow down the best not-so-pint-sized desserts at the Bahama Bucks Ol' Fashion Ice Cream Parlor, Ragan is scrolling through her phone.

"Everything okay?" I ask.

"Yeah, I'm sending a message to my Aunt Sophie. As soon as I walked in, she was out the door headed to a church meeting. I didn't have a chance to tell her I'd be going out. Not sure why I bother though. She isn't especially nice to me, but she dotes on CeeCee, so I guess I don't want her to worry."

"Mommy, Branch says I can have any size ice cream I want."

"I think what he meant to say is how much yummier the small sizes are. Right, Branch?"

"Yeah." I wink at Ragan, letting her know we're on the same page then I look back at Cecelia. "What your mom said."

"Loretta, this is Ragan and her daughter Cecelia."

"Hola. *Cómo estás*," Loretta says. And then with an excitement that catches me off guard, she pulls Ragan into a hug, Loretta's pregnant belly keeping them a fair distance apart. "It's so nice to meet you. I've heard a lot about you."

Confusion crosses Ragan's face and I glance at Jimmy, wondering what kind of spin he's put on my nonexistent friendship with Ragan.

"Nice to meet you, too, Loretta," Ragan replies.

Loretta goes about making introductions just as Dad pops in with Curtis, Jr. I hadn't expected him to bring the baby. But better he brings the baby than Charlene. Time with her is always uncomfortable for all involved. I can actually see Mama embracing *Dad* before forgiving the ex-best friend she once considered a sister.

The noise level increases as the group of family and friends becomes larger. Ragan releases her grasp of Cecelia who's quickly encircled by Tess, Tater, Isidora, and Luciana. After only seconds of chatter, the younger girls are running toward the toy room.

Ragan and Loretta fall into a conversation, and I figure whatever Ragan said to Loretta worked because they start to leave the room, Loretta talking ninety to nothing, her hands gesturing animatedly as she leads Ragan to the kitchen.

Ragan looks back at Jimmy who gives her a thumbs up and she smiles her response. The upturn of her lips seems to shift her entire appearance. She's not sullen or piping off a comeback at me, not paranoid or accusatory. She's just Ragan. And although she's admittedly unlike the chicks who tend to catch my eye, there's a uniqueness about her that grasps and holds my attention.

Is it only the physical? It has to be—that's the only type of relationship I allow with women. And with Ragan, well, I've eyed her rack so many times that I practically know her cup size. I know how her breasts look… without the shirt… without the bra. And my hands are the perfect size to grasp them whole, to squeeze them, to mark them.

She's what most would consider a big girl, but she's what I call curvy, and each curve perfectly accentuates her body. I watch the sway of her ass as she leaves the room. It's a great ass—the kind a man looks at with only one thing in mind—banging her from behind. I picture it so clearly. My pelvis slapping against that fuckable ass, each thrust harder and taking me deeper, slamming into her over and over. I can hear her moans as our naked bodies slap together at a vigorous speed. I can hear her crying out that she can't take anymore, but at the same time begging me not to stop. And I wouldn't. Not until her cunt is squeezing the come out of my dick. Yeah, that would be a nice start to driving away that attitude. And it would definitely chase away the sullenness.

With a full, round ass like hers, I'd bet fifty to nothing that the lips of her cunt are as plump as her upper lips. I can practically feel the slickness as my finger moves up and down her cleft, feel the warmth of her breath, the shivers that roll through her body and—

"Branch, did you hear me?" Jimmy asks, pulling me from the thoughts I shouldn't be having.

What the fuck? "Nope," I reply, sliding into a lie. "Sitting here wondering if Tucker will be able to increase the yardage of his passes in the next game."

Jimmy throws me a questioning glance and says, "Curtis and I are debating the odds of Dallas making it through the next round without you. What do you think?"

Jimmy's question launches a back and forth among the three of us until Ragan steps in and announces dinner's ready. When our eyes meet, I revisit my earlier thoughts. And heat rushes to her cheeks as if she can see the images running through my head. She looks away somewhat awkwardly and asks if she should go to the game room for Jace and his friend. I tell her I'll get them as the others head to the dining room.

When I return, everyone has been seated. Jace and Drake hurriedly grab seats on either side of Jimmy's oldest, Luciana, leaving the one chair next to Ragan empty. I take the seat and feel her stiffen beside me. I figured she'd be more at ease by now. Obviously not. But does it really matter if she's uncomfortable around me? Most women are, so why should she be any different? Seriously, what the fuck does it take for her to drop her guard? And why is it pissing me off that she hasn't?

She has no idea how fortunate she is. I could very well give her the same Branch McGuire that every other woman gets, and in less than five minutes she would be exactly as Carrie said—*horizontal*. Despite everything I've said and done, isn't that all I want anyway?

I glance at Ragan and she turns to meet my gaze. Those nervous brown eyes of hers meet the inquisitive blue of mine. That's when I decide that for some reason she *is* different and I leave it at that, not probing any deeper for fear of finding answers I don't wanna find.

Chapter
TWENTY-TWO

Ragan

HIS TENDER EXPRESSION MEETS THE ANXIOUS confusion of mine, and my stomach drops. I swallow hard, my eyes pressed to his as a flash of heat passes between us… and then nothing. His expression shifts, becoming hard and reserved, then he turns away before I can decipher anything further.

What was that? I return my attention to my surroundings and apply focus to everyone but him. Not an easy task considering the side of my body nearest his was seared by those mere seconds.

I engage in the table conversations, I laugh at the right moments, and I observe the others observing me. Particularly Jimmy and Loretta. Their eyes track from me to Branch and then to each other. Always in that sequence.

The evening continues to unravel, revealing the unexpected. Not only does the date versus nondate debacle continue, but a mass of nervous energy plays racquetball with my belly each time I look at Branch. So I try to keep my distance—sticking close to Loretta, storing the leftovers, helping with the dishes, tossing out elusive questions about Branch, and chatting her up about her unborn baby.

In return, she does her own digging, subtly inquiring about my relationship, or lack thereof, with Branch. I tell her what he told me—that he's just a guy being nice. And then I tell her I'm just a girl who took Jimmy up on a dinner offer that seemed like a great chance for CeeCee to make new friends. I don't tell her how I always feel naked under Branch's gaze. And there's no point telling her about the kitty purring or the panty poofing, so I avoid topics that'll lead to an inappropriate disclosure. As a matter of fact, I avoid any topic about Branch that could be misinterpreted. Especially since this isn't a date.

From across the room, I observe my daughter leaning over the arm of Branch's chair, looking on as he tickles his baby brother. And then Branch laughs when he hears the giggle he was aiming for. No sooner does my gaze settle on Branch do I perceive a difference. The change is mind-numbing. His arrogant subterfuge has faded. The star athlete persona has washed away. Every shield has been lowered and I feel as if I'm seeing the true *him*.

Could I have misjudged him? Could all the stories be wrong? Were the reporters and writers not given a chance to see this side of him?

When the baby begins to cry, Branch abruptly passes him to his Dad. Tess rushes over and woos CeeCee back to the pile of toys on the opposite side of the room. Before she grasps Tess's hand to leave, she gives Branch a hug. And at that moment, I realize that I *want* this to be a date.

Later, in the game room, or the ultimate man cave as Jimmy called it, he passes a beer to Branch and makes a joke about Branch having yet another admirer. I stop breathing until Jimmy clarifies, making it clear he was referencing CeeCee. The two men laugh, clink their bottles, and take long swigs of their beers. When Curtis joins the duo, I realize that it's difficult to determine which man is Branch's parent in this picture.

Branch and Jimmy resemble father and son in their gestures, but definitely not in their features. Branch towers over the curly-haired Jimmy, who's slender with dark eyes and obviously of Mexican descent. And then there's Curtis. He doesn't appear as easygoing with Branch as Jimmy, yet he bares the resemblance. Maybe a few inches taller than Branch. Similar builds and hair color. And similar brows offset by those piercing blue eyes.

Of course, Curtis is Branch's father, but if I had to judge solely on body language, Jimmy would be assigned that role. I wonder what the story is there. Because there's *definitely* a story. Did Curtis abandon his son? Is that why Branch said he knew what it felt like to have an absent father? Are the two finally reconnecting, hence the celebratory dinner?

Although the evening started with a gross misjudgment on my part, it's easily transitioned to something else. Something that feels oddly comforting while still capturing all the discomforts of a first date. I first noticed it with CeeCee. Branch was so sweet and kind and attentive to her at the ice cream parlor and still now at Loretta and Jimmy's. And she seems to have taken to him, which is unlike her. It normally takes awhile for her to warm up to *anyone*.

Branch looks up from the pool table and catches me eyeing him. He flashes a grin and tips his chin. I glance over my shoulder thinking his gesture was meant for someone else. But no one's around; it's only me. I point at myself and mouth, *me*. Branch mouths *yes*, *you* and gives me a wink. I blush. There he goes again, doing something simple that feels *everything* but simple to me.

That wink, for instance. Not only does it flutter my heart, but it speaks to kitty. It's a hello that yields soft purrs and insta-wetness. I try to think it away, to settle into the heat of his gaze, but kitty keeps purring and the wet gets wetter. I shift uncomfortably in my seat as my insides pulse under the guise of an impending climax. Oh, sweet fuck, who is he? The Kitty Whisperer?

"Looks like you can't keep your eyes off the obnoxious guy you claim is less than a friend," Loretta says, interrupting whatever crazy thing is happening between Branch and me.

I pull my gaze away from the spellbindingly hot man who has just earned the title of Kitty Whisperer. "Just because I'm looking in that direction doesn't mean I'm looking at Branch."

"Yes, they're handsome guys, but I doubt you were checking out Jimmy or Curtis."

"Okay, you win. But not about the keeping my eyes off of him part. I was looking at him because I'm trying to figure him out," I lie. Well, it isn't entirely untrue. I *am* trying to get a read on him.

Loretta passes a hand over her belly. She sure looks further along than seven months. And she's positively radiant—she wears pregnancy well. And I can see why they're on child number five. Loretta is a vibrant, beautiful, and sexy woman. I'm sure Jimmy can't keep his hands off her.

"Hmm," she muses and looks toward Branch. "I don't think he's hard to figure out."

"For you maybe."

"Well, he's like a son to me, so that's probably true," she says. "But it's quite simple actually."

"Simple? Branch McGuire? Somehow I doubt that."

"You're thinking there are two of him, aren't you?" She takes a seat across from me at the card table.

"Well, yeah."

"There's only one," she says. "And you're looking at him."

"But the cocky asshole that I typically see, who's that guy?"

She laughs and waves my question away. "That's a guy being a guy. Some men have an overabundance of confidence, especially if they have a few advantages like Branch. But they also have insecurities, like you and me. And also like you and me, they have shields. Maybe that confidence is his."

"CeeCee, you know better. Apologize to her."

She looks up at Tess. "I'm sorry."

"Now give her dolly back."

Tess grabs her doll from CeeCee and runs from the room.

I grasp Cecelia by the shoulders and turn her toward me.

"You don't take things that don't belong to you. Do you understand?"

"But I want it."

"Cecelia, that was Tess's doll. Not yours. You were wrong to take it. Now, tell me you understand."

"No," she says, her lips moving into a pout.

Aunt Sophie mentioned that CeeCee had been misbehaving at the church nursery, taking things that didn't belong to her and throwing a tantrum when her behavior was corrected. So when she yanks away from me, I've pretty much decided on spanking her bottom. But one look in her eyes and I know I can't do it. I can *never* do it. Even when she needs it. She looks at me as if daring me to do or say anything further. When tears sting my eyes, I resign and send CeeCee off to play with Tess.

I stare after her, knowing my baby girl will need discipline, and sometimes that will be in the form of a spanking, but I can't do that to her. I can't be that person. But how can I be an effective parent without rendering discipline?

"Everything okay?"

I wipe my cheeks and look up as Branch approaches. I don't want another mother-daughter showdown with CeeCee. Especially not here. *It's time to go.*

"Yeah." I go to grab CeeCee's backpack. "Can you take us home?" I ask, averting my eyes.

"I thought you were having a good time. Did something happen?"

"I upheld my part of the bargain. Now I want to go. If you won't take me, I'll call Hayley." I go for my purse and he grasps my arm.

"Hey, I'll take you," he says, confusion plastered over his face. "Just let me tell them we're leaving."

"Is something wrong?" Loretta asks when I trail into the room minutes later.

"CeeCee is acting out and I want to get her home and into bed," I say, my voice small, my spirit broken. "Thanks for having us."

"Of course. And thanks for helping out," Loretta adds. "You're welcome to come by anytime. The girls loved playing with Cecelia."

"Thanks," I say. But I don't suspect I'll be coming back.

"So what did I do *this* time to upset you?" Branch asks as we make the first turn leaving Jimmy's.

"You didn't do anything." It never occurred to me that he may have misinterpreted my rush to leave.

"Did someone else upset you?"

I can't tell him the truth. That I didn't want anyone at Jimmy's to see me lose my shit. Especially him. The last time CeeCee faced a spanking, I chickened out then, too. Ended up sitting on the floor, my arms wrapped around my knees, rocking myself and crying like a freaking baby as visions of my past flashed in my head. I was that seven-year-old kid again. And I was helpless. Screaming for Dad as Cassidy did her worst—slapping me across the face, shoving me to the floor, ordering me to pull my panties down so she could whip my bare ass with a belt. Or with her shoe. Or with whatever she could get ahold of. She'd said she never wanted to hurt her hands. But to my body, she rendered every bit of hurt that she could. And when she let loose, she didn't have the capacity to stop. Each time, she lost control. And my body was evidence of that lapse. She'd given welts and bruises I'd had to cover for years.

I don't want to become Cassidy. I don't want to be the

mom who loses control. How can I tell Branch any of this without him looking at me with pity? Or worse, seeing me as some nutcase? With Ethan, it had been easier because we'd both come from abusive homes. He could relate and understand. But not Branch. There's no way he would. So I take the path I've most often traveled—lies and denial.

"It's nothing like that. And no, I don't want to talk about it."

Branch exhales his frustration. "You won't hear another word from me."

That sounded permanent. As if he's not only done with the subject at hand, but with me altogether.

Chapter
TWENTY-THREE

Branch

"THANKS FOR ARRANGING THIS, SON," DAD SAYS and follows me to the living room.

"Have a seat and I'll let her know you're here." I step out of the room, wondering if I've done the right thing. Mama was certainly happy when I told her Dad wanted to see her. I mean, all of the anger and the supposed *hate* disappeared in a puff of smoke, and her face took on an expression I've *never* seen.

I'd initially chosen to disregard Dad's request to see Mama, but he asked again. Before deciding either way, I checked with Christina to see how things were going with the routinely uncooperative patient—same as I do every day. She reported Mama was doing well—taking her meds without issue and even being a little less rude to her. Her update paralleled the doc's reports and was also on track with what I'd seen for myself. If nothing else, confirmation of Mama's continued improvement relieves the pressure I've been managing, which means I'll be leaving Blue Ridge sooner than I expected. And *that* means I won't miss the final playoff game. I'm amped at the thought of being on the field again—the crowd at my back, the adrenaline running through my veins—there's nothing like it.

I run into Christina in the hallway that leads to Mama's bedroom. When I tell her Dad's here, she volunteers to let Mama know, so I do an about-face—all the while, second-guessing this ill-advised rendezvous and mentally preparing myself for just about *anything*.

"This is nice, Branch. Real nice," Dad says, marveling at his surroundings when I reenter the room. "This is a good thing you did for your mama."

"It's what she's always wanted," I say when he turns to look at me. "I remember the day I brought her here and told her it was hers. She cried for hours." Now I wonder if those tears were only about the house. Could they have been for the hopes and dreams of the life she'd lost?

"Yep, it's exactly as she described years and years ago… when we were just starting out," he says, avoiding my eyes.

I sense that he, too, is emotional over the dreams that never came to be. Thankfully, I don't have much time to deliberate on his reaction because Mama steps into the room, and my eyes nearly pop out of my head.

"Hello, Curtis," she says.

Dad turns to face Mama. He doesn't speak. He merely looks at her. And she, in turn, moves her eyes slowly over him. And then, as if on cue, they step closer, and before I know it, their bodies are pressed together in an embrace. *What the hell?*

They cling to one another for way longer than any hug should ever be. When I clear my throat not once, but twice, they finally release each other and place a fairly decent amount of space between themselves.

My eyes dart back to Mama who looks nothing like *my* mama. I've always thought of her as pretty, but today she looks like one of those hot cougar bombshells who throw themselves at me during the postgame parties. She's beautiful. Her dress is a little tighter than it should be. *She'll hear my opinion on that later.* Her long brown hair, which is typically pulled back, cascades around her face, and she's wearing *that* necklace. The one I was damn near torched and burned for even asking about when I was a child and still now as an adult. *What the hell?*

"Why don't we have a seat," I suggest, trying to diffuse the chemistry between them. "Mama, you can sit in the chair and I'll take the couch with Dad."

"Branch, weren't you and Jace heading out to that ice cream parlor you two like so much?" Mama asks as she sits on the couch beside Dad—a total disregard for my seating plan.

"Uh… yeah, but you were going, too, remember?" It's not like her to pass up spending time with me.

"I must have forgotten to tell you that I changed my mind," she says, eyeing me with an expression I don't quite understand.

Is she trying to get rid of me?

"You can bring back my usual two scoops of chocolate," she adds, confirming that she *is* trying to get rid of me. Well, tough shit because I ain't leaving.

"I'll wait," I reply, my eyes pasted to Dad, who's gaping at Mama the same way those cougars eye me. "In case you need something."

"What can I possibly need, Branch?" Mama asks.

"Besides, Christina's here. Go on now. Give your daddy and me some time alone. We have years of catching up to do."

The sit-down has only started and it's already going off the rails. "Mama, leaving you here alone is not what I had in mind when I arranged this."

"I'll be fine. Don't I look fine to you?"

Hell, she looks unrecognizable.

My eyes flick back to Dad's and then to the small space on the couch between Mama and him. He's holding her hand. *What the hell?* I have so many questions that I can't manage to get even one of them out.

"I'll take good care of Mary," he says. "You have my word."

Jace comes bounding down the stairs yelling for me.

"In here, Jace!" I shout back, my eyes never leaving Curtis and Mary McGuire.

"Dad!" my brother exclaims, upon entering the room. He runs past me to our father and inserts himself between my parents on the couch. Dad tousles his hair as Mama looks on with a smile.

I'm looking at the picture-perfect family. But everyone here knows we're not a *normal* family, so what the actual fuck?

My gaze moves over my dad, my mama, and finally my brother.

Everyone is alive with excitement. Everyone except me.

Because I know where this can lead.

To a dark hole that will consume us all.

Dad's car is still in the driveway when Jace and I return from the parlor. I kick myself for letting Mama convince me to go without her. I should have insisted they meet someplace else. Maybe at the shrink's. He could have managed any possible meltdowns. But now, as it stands, if Dad says or does anything to set Mama off, it's all on my shoulders.

Jace heads to the game room—per my instructions—and I go to the kitchen to place Mama's ice cream in the freezer. Having decided it's time for Dad's visit to come to an end, I walk to the living room, but aside from two coffee cups on the table, there's no sign of them. I go to the patio—Mama likes to sit out there and listen to the wind chimes. But Dad and Mama aren't there either. I remember how Dad was looking around the house—maybe Mama's giving him a tour. I go back inside and check the rooms we normally show. Still no sign of my parents.

The warning I've carried all afternoon screeches in my head. I practically run down the hallway and when I go to knock on Mama's door, it opens before I have a chance. And one look at Dad and I know all I need to.

"Where's Mama?" I demand, my anger already in tow.

"Branch, I thought you'd be gone longer," I hear her say, her voice floating across the room.

I shove the door open wider and rake my eyes over her disheveled appearance. A sense of betrayal seeps through every part of me. "Yeah, well I can see that. Mama, what the hell are you doing?"

Sliding from the bed, she grabs her robe and rushes to my side. I can already see the explanation on her lips. And I know there isn't one that she can give me that I'll accept. She astutely gauges my demeanor and then rests a calming hand on my forearm.

"Don't." That's all I say and she jerks her hand away as if she's been burned.

"Branch. Son, I know how this must look," Dad says, his voice uneasy.

I turn on a heel to face him, disbelief and anger fueling my insides. "It *looks* like you came over here to lay down some bullshit and then fuck my mama."

Mama pushes between us, her hand connecting hard and fast with my cheek, the clap of it echoing across the room.

I flinch and jerk my head back.

"Don't you dare speak that way about your father or me! Do you hear me, Branch McGuire?"

I meet her eyes, knowing she sees the rage in mine. I don't know what the fuck to think or who to blame. *Fuck.* Maybe it's my fault—I'm the one who allowed this to happen.

Same as earlier, they move as if on cue, turning away from me and losing themselves in each other's gaze like two star-crossed lovers. Part of me wants to tell them both to go to hell and the other part is confused as shit.

I have to put an end to this before it goes any further. I won't let Dad destroy what little sanity Mama has left. "What the hell, Dad?"

"This isn't why I wanted to see Mary." He holds out his hands, palms up. "I love your mother. I've never stopped. And I know I never will." He stares at me, torment flashing in his eyes before he recovers.

"So, you love my mother, but you're going home to another woman's bed? To Mama's *best friend's* bed?" My hands fist at my sides, shaking with barely contained anger. "You think that's okay?"

"That whore is no friend of mine," Mama says.

"But this guy is?" I ask, pointing at Dad.

"Branch," she says, taking a careful step toward me. "He's my husband."

Those words tear the last of my restraint, and anger overtakes me. "Your *husband*? So now you finally tell me? Well, where was your husband when we were sitting in the dark eating fucking peanut butter sandwiches?"

"Branch, please. That was my fault. Let me get myself together and we can all sit down and talk." Mama closes her robe and smoothes a hand over her hair.

"Whatever sick shit you two have going on"—I wave my hands, indicating I'm out—"I don't even want to know."

Dad snatches my arm as I walk past, but I jerk from his grasp. "And when she goes batshit crazy on you, don't come looking for me."

"Branch! Wait! Please!" Mama yells after me, her voice breaking as she starts to cry.

I tune her out and head for Jace, making sure he doesn't walk into the same shit I did.

Chapter
TWENTY-FOUR

Ragan

I T'S LUNCH HOUR—THE TIME I USUALLY HAVE A RUN-IN with Branch. And of all the days I don't want to see him, this one tops the list. I'm uneasy about everything— looking at him, greeting him, taking his order—you name it and I don't want to do it. My stomach churns and I literally feel ill. And when I *do* look at him, it'll only be worse because all I'll see is that disaster of an evening at Jimmy's. And if it *was* a date… epic fail. Those last moments with him were an endless stretch of awkward silence. The kind that makes you want to disappear into thin air.

I'd been out sick the last couple of days, but upon arriving at work this morning, Carrie was quick to tell me that Branch had come in the last two days, arriving exactly at noon. She says it was obvious he was coming in for me. I told her I doubted it, and that I didn't care either way. But here I am—looking, waiting, and caring.

I step from behind the counter, expecting Branch to stroll in and sit at his usual table. And like clockwork, the door opens, and in he walks. *The Man on Fire*, full of swagger, confidence, and just hellafied hot, but this time he's not alone. He's with that crowd of friends again—the Quad. He doesn't head for his usual table either.

Branch looks up, grinning broadly until his eyes catch mine. It's only for a second and he turns away, pointing toward a table on the opposite side of the diner—in Carrie's station. Oh, joy! *She's going to love that!* Pretending it's no big deal, I busy myself with my other tables. My heart sinks a little though, which comes as a shock. I should be relieved, but something inside me indicates otherwise. I exhale a sigh. If I were a hashtag, it would definitely be *confused*.

I try not to, but I find myself sneaking a glance across the diner. And as expected, Carrie is in full flirt mode. She's unbuttoned her shirt to reveal even more cleavage if that were at all possible. She was bursting out of her top as it was. I've said it before, and I'll say it again—it's hard to believe she's married. The way she carries on, you'd swear she's a hooker. She's even let her hair down, one of Jim Bob's big no-no's. Her shoulder-length ashen-blond curls spring to life as much as she does. She tosses her head back and laughs, leaning over to pass one of the guys a menu, her bosoms practically touching his head. *Boy, is she proud of those tits.* She saved tips for three years to cover half the cost of the boob job, her husband paid the other half, and is she ever getting her money's worth.

"Ragan."

I blink from my daze and turn to my boss's frowning disapproval. "Are you going to daydream or work?" He gestures toward the group sitting at one of my tables.

"Sorry." *Shit.* This man must think I'm a total fucktard.

Nearly an hour and several customers later, I step from

the kitchen and see Branch talking to Jim Bob, undoubtedly complaining about me. That would explain why he didn't sit at his regular table.

I stare until Branch looks up and catches me focused on him. He has the nerve to smile. *Is he kidding me?* Of course I don't return the gesture. I go about my business—giving the couple in the *Little Richard* booth their check and wondering if the end of the day will find me jobless.

Grabbing my tip from the adjacent booth, I stuff the bills into my apron and start prepping the area for the next customer. But almost as if they have no choice, my eyes find their way back to Branch. His buddies are gone now, and he's still talking to my boss.

I'm certain Jim Bob's getting a rundown of every unflattering remark I've sounded off at Branch. Not to mention the mistakes I've made. Why else would Branch talk to Jim Bob for any length of time? There can only be one reason—Branch is trying to get me fired. Is this how he handles things with women when he doesn't get his way? But I would imagine that *never* happens. I'm probably the only crazy exception. And even now, in these fucked circumstances, I look at him and damn if kitty doesn't purr. *The Kitty Whisperer strikes again.* I hate it and crave it all at the same time. I'm one big ball of confusion with a fucked-up past that has a choke hold on my life. And Branch only adds to that confusion. I mean, why would he help me on one end and then hurt me on the other? He knows I need this job. *Fucking asshat.* Yeah, he's definitely a confusion I don't need. If losing this job means getting rid of him, I'm all for it.

I have the good mind to walk over and tell him to kiss

where the sun doesn't shine. As a matter of fact, I will. I take a few misguided steps in their direction—my shoulders squared, my temper rising and my mind set on telling them both to kiss off. But then, good sense kicks in and I make a beeline to the counter. Although I don't act like it, I can't afford to lose this job and I can't risk blowing my top in front of Jim Bob, even with a customer like Branch who deserves every bit of attitude he's gotten from me.

My customer Mel beckons for another cup of the hot muddy Georgia water that Jim Bob passes off as coffee. I reach for the coffee pot and notice that although Carrie has somehow managed to abandon Branch's immediate vicinity, she's still eyeing him like a piece of meat. And unlike her previous ogling sessions, this time it pulls at an emotion that I have no right to—an emotion I wish I didn't have.

Pushing past my irritation with Carrie, I give attention to Mel who's awaiting his coffee refill.

"Can I get this to go?" he asks, looking up from his near-empty plate.

"Sure," I reply and move toward the carry-out cups. I step past Carrie, who's yet to move. "If you stare any harder, you'll go blind."

She lets out a sigh and shakes her head. "That is one fine-looking man. And that body, it's enough to give a woman the kind of orgasm that will land her in the hospital. *And* he's rich! Why would you go and mess that up? For girls like us, he's a once-in-a-lifetime opportunity."

Girls like us? Does she not realize how old she is?

I ignore her comment. "You asked for his autograph again, didn't you? Who did you tell him it was for this time? Your unborn nephew?"

She laughs. "I don't know what you have against the guy, Ragan."

"Here you go, Mel." I pass him the coffee and his check as I reply to Carrie. "I don't have anything against him. But I hate that he walks in here like he's the best thing happening."

"Well in this town, he is. And just because you refuse to acknowledge it, that doesn't mean the rest of us have to," she says. "And good idea about getting an autograph for little Levi. He's due next month." She tears a piece of paper from her pad and hurries over to Branch and Jim Bob.

I place a lid on Ronnie's cup of lemonade and set it on the counter. After altering his check, I head back to his table. Ronnie says he'll see me tomorrow, makes some joke that I don't quite understand, and scarfs down the last of his sandwich.

I follow the sound of the door chime, catching a glimpse of Branch as he exits the diner. An uneasy breath escapes my lungs and I chastise myself for letting this get so deeply under my skin. But it has… and for so many different reasons. And Carrie's right. A guy like Branch—showing the least bit of interest, even if it was only to get a rise out of me—is a once-in-a-lifetime opportunity. And I blew it.

"Ragan."

I look up from preparing the napkins and silverware. "Yes?"

"Can you come to my office?" Jim Bob asks.

Oh shit. "Yeah, sure. Let me get this check to the *Elvis Booth* and I'll be right there." This is it. I'm about to be raked over the coals or possibly fired altogether. *Fucking Branch.*

I pass the check and napkins to my customer and head back to Jim Bob's office. He's sitting at his desk, typing away.

Probably jacking up the prices on the slop he passes off as food. Maybe I should come back later. At least try to get some more tips before he throws me out on my ass. He looks up right as I decide to leave.

"Ragan, don't just stand there. Come in."

"You looked busy. I didn't want to interrupt."

"I asked to see you, remember? Have a seat."

Oh hell. Yep, I'm getting fired. But why sit me down? Say it and get it over with. I can hear Aunt Sophie now. *I practically threw that job in your lap and you lose it already. A five-year-old can take orders and wait tables. What is wrong with you, Ragan? Are you determined to be a loser all your life?*

"This is for you," Jim Bob says and passes an envelope to me.

A letter of termination? Why so formal all of a sudden? With trembling fingers, I open the envelope, surprised by the contents nestled inside. Three crisp hundred-dollar bills.

"What's this for?" I ask, thinking it's the last of my wages.

"It's a tip from a customer. He said he'd been skimping you and wanted to set things right and—"

"And what?" I ask, looking up from the envelope.

"That you were a great waitress and I was lucky to have you."

"Really?" I wasn't a *great* waitress to anyone. That much I know. And judging from Jim Bob's doubtful expression, he knows it's bullshit, too.

Noting my confusion, he adds, "It's from our resident football star."

I glance back at the three bills in my hand.

Branch did this?

#confused

Chapter
TWENTY-FIVE

Branch

"WHEN YOU SAID YOU WERE TAKING THE boat out, you didn't mention the two of them," I scowl at Dad and Mama sitting at the rear of the pontoon boat. "What the hell are they doing here?"

Jimmy steps in front of me, blocking my path. "Let 'em be, Branch. Just let 'em be."

I pull my gaze from my parents and glare at Jimmy. "So all of a sudden you're Team Curtis and Mary?"

"Haven't I always looked out for you? Why would I stop now?"

"Then why are you encouraging this?" I ask, gesturing toward my parents. "What are you doing?"

"Still looking out for you," he replies, his voice filled with empathy and understanding. "You may not see that right now, but in time you will."

Jimmy's girls and their friends take the short jump from the dock to the boat, and Jimmy and I move out of earshot toward the cabin.

"Jimmy, I'm barely processing what I've learned already. What's next? How much more shit will I have to put up with?" I ask, in a hushed tone.

"Curtis came to me after you and I talked."

I exhale a sigh and shove my fingers through my hair. "Oh, yeah? And what load of bull did he dump on you this time?"

"In a nutshell, he told me he still loves Mary."

I fall quiet, restraining the ire and staring at the lake, watching as a smaller boat sails past us. "He's a fucking liar and a cheater. Why would you believe a word that comes out of his mouth?"

Jimmy leans in and whispers, "The man was in tears, Branch. And I ain't talking about the random tear down a cheek. He was full-out crying."

I turn back to face Jimmy. "Why now? Why not way back then when we needed him? Regardless of how much shit Mama put him through. Why give up on someone you love as much as he *claims* to love Mama? And don't get me started on her." I shake my head, disgusted by Mama's behavior. "She made my dad public enemy number one for over half my life and now she goes and pulls this shit. Did I tell you that she slapped me? She fucking slapped me because I called Dad out on his bullshit!"

"Branch, we both know they've made some mistakes they can't come back from, but it looks like they're finally trying to get their acts together. No one said it was gonna be easy, but to fight whatever they're trying to fix only makes it that much harder on you. I thought you got that. I thought you'd decided to be the bigger person."

"Fuck that. I'm tired of being the bigger person. Mama

has relied on me for everything. *Every* fucking thing. Do you have any idea what that does to a kid?" I ask, the anger already taking hold of me. "Or how it fucks with my head even now? I'm the one who's been here for years, but dear old Dad swoops in for one day and she's on her back and then slapping the shit out of me for demanding he have more respect for her than that. She always said it was me and her against the world. *Me and her*! But she throws all those years out the window in *one* afternoon for some dick she's basically sharing with her best friend."

Jimmy shakes his head, his brown eyes revealing that same depth of compassion he's displayed over the years for the scorned boy who's become a man. "Branch, I know you're pissed and I know it's tearing you up inside, but don't say things like that about your parents."

"You know what? Fuck this. I'm outta here." I turn on a heel to abandon ship but come face-to-face with Ragan and Cecelia. *What the hell are they doing here?*

I whip around at Jimmy. "What are you trying to do to me, man?"

Jimmy holds up his hands in defense. "Take it up with the wife. She thought it would be good to get the girls together again. Tess liked playing with Cecelia, but Loretta doubted Ragan would let her come alone."

Not wanting to step toward my parents, Jimmy, or Ragan, I feel that burn again, as if my insides are about to explode. I need to get the hell away from all of them. Before I make a step either way, Ragan's little girl is running toward me. She comes to a stop and tugs at my pant leg. I look down at her. The flames that swept through me are somehow instantly smothered by the innocence of her smile.

I reach down and lift her into my arms. "Hey, pretty girl."

"Hi, Branch," she says and extends her arms around my neck.

"Are you here for more ice cream?" I whisper.

She pulls back and looks at me, her head bobbing up and down.

"Come on, CeeCee," Tess yells.

Cecelia pushes away from me, a signal for me to release her. And I comply. As soon as her feet hit the floor, she and Tess are off, squealing and laughing.

Jimmy tips his head toward Ragan. "Glad you could make it."

"Me too. It's an unseasonably nice day."

"You know what they say about Georgia weather," he says, looking over Ragan's head. "I need to go help the wife." He's gone before either of us can reply.

"And then there were two," I say and step closer to Ragan.

"Hey, Branch," she says, her voice meek, almost bashful, and so unlike the Ragan I'm accustomed to.

"Sup, sugar."

"Sorry about the other night," she says, shaking her head. "I was dealing with… some crap from my past."

I shrug. "Happens to the best of us." I glance at my parents and grit my teeth.

"And I just wanted to say thanks for the—"

"Don't mention it," I say, looking down at her, knowing she's referring to my tip.

Her lips part to say more, but I cut her off again when I see Christina. "Hey, I'll catch up with you later," I say and leave her standing alone.

"Why is Mama here?" I ask, grasping Christina's arm,

pulling her away from the others.

When she meets the anger in my expression, her smile fades. "I didn't know it would be a problem. Mary said Jimmy was like family to you."

"And because of that, you didn't think to run this by me?"

"I… uh," she starts, confusion crossing her face. "I've taken Mary out before, so I figured this was okay."

"I don't pay you to figure out shit. I pay you to do as you're told. Shit like this, I need to know about—you got it?"

"I'm sorry. I haven't seen Mary this excited in, well, ever. And I thought a day on the lake would be good for her." Her voice drops to a low whisper. "I didn't mean to upset you."

Fuck. She looks scared shitless. I exhale a sigh and attempt to suppress what's still trying to build. "It's all right. But anything other than medical visits or errands, run it by me first. At least while I'm here."

"While you're here? So you're getting ready to leave Blue Ridge?" she asks, not bothering to hide the disappointment in her voice. "I was hoping for a chance to get to know you better."

Get to know me better? Ha, that's code for *please, fuck me.* My eyes roam over her tight little body. As usual, she doesn't disappoint. She's wearing a low-cut V-neck T-shirt that outlines the curves of her breasts and painted-on skinny jeans. And by painted on, I mean form-fitting ripped jeans that expose so much skin, you can't help but want to rip away the remainder of the denim to get to what's underneath. My gaze shifts to the cloth that barely covers her tits and I watch as her nipples tighten into pebbles. Why *haven't* I fucked her yet? *Because it's too close to home, Branch.* Too close to what matters most. But hell, why should I give a fuck now? I nearly smile when I think about Mama's request that I keep *Little Branch* away from Christina. But then I remember that my Mama and I are *not* my Mama and I anymore. So it looks like little Miss Christina is about to get a very *large* Branch.

I lean in close and whisper, "I won't be gentle."

"Who says I want you to be?" she challenges, stepping closer to me.

Before I respond, I hear the laughter of the one guy who will make a day with Curtis and Mary almost bearable. And he isn't alone. My boys!

"Is this why you've been ignoring our calls?" Matt asks, moving his eyes appreciatively over Christina. "I'm Matt." He reaches for her hand and places it to his lips with a kiss.

"Don't be an ass," I say and disconnect their hands. After introducing the guys to Christina, we grab some beers, head to the upper deck, and flip on the music.

"Isn't that the waitress from that diner you can't seem to stay away from?" Matt asks when he spots Ragan.

"Yeah, that's her," I say. "Why?"

"I don't know how I didn't notice before, but she's pretty hot." He takes a sip of his beer.

"Oh, yeah?" I ask, attempting nonchalance.

"Hell, yeah," he says and makes a step in her direction.

My hand clutches his shoulder, holding him in place. "Stay away from her." The words come out as a warning, escaping my lips before I know it.

Matt eyes me, and I know he senses something is off, but I also know he won't challenge me. "No problem, bro."

Throughout the day, I barely acknowledge Ragan, but our eyes meet enough to carry on a conversation that should happen but never does. I catch her watching me with Christina, who conveniently fell into my lap on more than one occasion. And I catch her watching me fuck off with the fellas, but she doesn't approach me, nor do I go to her.

As the sun lowers on the horizon, the boat U-turns and the under-deck lighting flips on, illuminating the dark water with a blueish glow while the pontoon's interior is brightened by the iridescent bulbs that hang overhead. Their dim firefly lights seem to deepen the pulse of the music traveling over the speaker system.

By now, the slow burn incited by Curtis and Mary is fleeting. It's the alcohol. I've had more than my share but still I indulge. As my beer tally rises, my better judgment moves to the recesses of my mind, and my attention is diverted from Christina to Ragan and back to Christina again.

She keeps a watchful eye on Mama while still doing her best to keep me on a string, making it clear to anyone who gets too close that she's the evening's conquest. I find it amusing that she thinks she actually has it like that, but I don't object. I let her have her fun. But Ragan watches that, too. I read women well enough to recognize the eye of jealousy, so I know she doesn't like what she sees.

I slide Christina from my lap and head down to the lower deck for more beer. I hit the last step, and one of the two people I'd managed to avoid till now is standing in front of me. My first instinct is to punch him square in the face.

"I'm sorry," Dad says, his words catching me off guard.

I don't reply. I can't. My focus is on not letting him get another rise out of me.

"I know you've gotten my messages. How long are you going to avoid me?"

"For as long as you were out of my life. And that doesn't

even begin to make us even."

"Can I have a few minutes?" he asks.

"We have nothing to talk about."

"I've come so close to having you back in my life. Please, son."

Looks as if I'm gonna join Mama and Dad on that trip to Crazyville, because I actually want to hear what he thinks he can possibly say to make any of this shit right. Opening the door to the cabin, I step inside and he follows.

I lean against the wet bar with my legs and arms crossed. "So talk."

"I know everything is a mess, but I'm taking steps to set things right," he says, in a rush.

"Like what? Fucking one desperate woman instead of two?"

"Branch, don't," he starts and takes a deep breath, obviously forcing himself to ignore my jab. "I want to be with your mother."

"What about Charlene?"

He shakes his head and lets out a sigh. "That relationship." He shakes his head again. "It never should have happened."

"But it did. Of all the women, why her? Why Mama's best friend?"

"It wasn't planned if that's what you're thinking. That day when Mary had pushed my last button, I was sitting in the driveway trying to come up with something I hadn't already tried that would get through to her. Sometime later, Charlene pulled up, saw me in the car, got in, and we started talking. She told me if I wanted her couch for a couple of nights, it was mine. Those couple of nights became a week, and that's when she offered her spare room. And I took it. Figured it would give me some time to sort stuff out. Let Mary cool off."

"How did that work out for you?" I ask, knowing full well it didn't.

"You know Mary. Once she gets something in her head, she runs with it. When a neighbor told her I was living with Charlene, Mary did a little recon of her own. But everything she saw was circumstantial—there was nothing sexual between Charlene and me. Not in the least. Day after day, I tried to talk to your mama, but she wouldn't hear me out. She'd become erratic and accusatory, so I'd leave. And then one day, your mama called Charlene who verified I'd been staying with her, but before Charlene could tell her the whole story, Mary called her a backstabbing whore and hung up. From there, Mary drew her own conclusions."

"And you let her. Guess you figured it was best to wait a decade or so to straighten that out."

He looks down as if ashamed. "I'm not gonna lie. The peace and quiet at Charlene's looked a lot better than what I had going on at home. And the longer I stayed, the more convinced Mary became that I was sleeping with Charlene."

"What did you expect? And if it was all so innocent, how did CJ come into the picture? Immaculate conception?"

"After a while, it just happened," he says, his voice low. "There was no discussion. We fell into being a couple."

"And you were both okay with that? You cheating and her sleeping with her best friend's husband?"

"It wasn't like that. I lost a wife and she lost a friend. We attempted to comfort each other and one thing led to another. And Charlene knew—she knew I still loved Mary, but she was willing to take what little of me I could give her at the time. And to be honest, being around her made me feel as though I still had a part of Mary. As the years ticked by, my feelings for Mary didn't change and I wanted to tell Charlene that my heart was still with someone else. But how could I tell her that? Who wants to hear that type of shit, Branch? That I was using her to fill a void? I couldn't do it."

I shake my head. "And now, years later—after God knows how many hours of therapy, not to mention the abandonment and relationship issues you've caused—you want to step up to the plate and finally be a man?"

Dad steps forward, the unrestrained emotion evident in his gaze. "Look, son. There's only so much of your disrespect I'm gonna take."

I don't falter, staring him directly in the eyes with the same unharnessed fervor, daring him to take a step closer. For long moments, we engage in an unspoken challenge until he finally lets out a breath and continues.

"I've always wanted to step up to the plate, as you phrase it. But I couldn't make someone do something they refused to do, dammit," he says, his voice cracking. "You know how Mary can be when she's off her meds, don't you? Well, imagine her not medicated, angry, *and* vengeful. That's what I was dealing with."

He takes a few paces toward me, but I step to the side.

"Things are different now. We know how to keep Mary being *Mary*," he says. "And I've told Charlene everything. She was hurt—as to be expected. But she said she's known all along that she'd only filled a small corner of my heart. She said she wants to see me happy. And I want the same for her. Maybe now, we can all have that."

Having decided I've heard enough, my eyes lock with his as I cock my head to the side. "So everyone is falling in line except me. Well, if you were hoping this talk would change anything, it did. I'm even more convinced that you're a piece of shit."

Hurt flashes in his eyes as his shoulders drop.

"Thanks for the chat, Pops," I say and leave him in the cabin staring after me.

"Goodbye, Cecelia."

"Ice cream tomorrow," she whispers.

I look at Ragan. "That's up to your mom."

"Come on, sweetie, it's time to go. Say goodbye to Branch," Ragan says, reaching for her daughter.

It's as if she can't get away from me fast enough. I pass Cecelia to her and say, "I overheard you telling Loretta you have the early shift tomorrow. The part Jimmy ordered arrives in the morning, so your car should be ready by late afternoon. I'll pick you up for work."

"That's okay, I don't—"

"I'm picking you up," I say with an air of authority that catches her off guard.

Before either of us says another word, Christina saunters over, not bothering to acknowledge Ragan. "Branch, I'll get your mom settled at home and then we have that really *hard* game to finish." Christina grasps my hand, urging me to follow her, but I pull back. The only woman's hand I've ever held is Mama's.

As I step away from Ragan, something pulls at me and I

glance over my shoulder. Although she was in a rush to place distance between the two of us, Ragan has yet to move. She stands in place, staring after me. And even though each step takes me farther away, it feels like a part of me is still standing there with her and Cecelia.

THE END

BRANCH AND RAGAN'S STORY CONTINUES
IN THE SEQUEL

Salvaged
HEARTS

no longer broken duet
book two

A Snippet from Salvaged Hearts

Ragan

"Hold the ball like this… with your fingers bent like so." Branch holds the football in front of me and then rotates it three hundred and sixty degrees. "See?"

"Yeah."

"And when you throw it, don't just toss it any kind of way," he says and grins down at me. "Throw with a purpose. Have a target."

"Okay." Maybe I should make *him* my target. "I've got it."

"Good. And lose the attitude. We can't let a group of preteens kick our asses."

"But it's six of them," Hayley says.

"I more than make up for the whole lot of 'em, but you guys have to do something."

Hayley laughs and I toss her a frustrated glance.

"Go out a few feet and let's see if Ragan can manage to get it in your direction this time."

"Whatever," I say and grab the ball from him. I position myself to throw the ball and he stops me again.

"Spread your feet and angle back like I've shown you."

I mimic his example and he shakes his head. Stepping behind me, his hand is on my midsection and I tense. I hate that part of my body and I sure as hell don't want the likes of Branch McGuire touching it, more than likely comparing it to the abdominal muscles he's used to, those that aren't hidden by a layer of unnecessary insulation. I go to move his hand, but he resists.

"Relax, sugar," he says. His breath is warm against my cheek and his foot is positioned between mine as he whispers instructions in my ear. I don't take in a damn thing he says. I'm picturing those full perfect lips and how close they are to my face. If he leans in just a couple of inches more, his mouth would be on my skin. I tell myself to zero in on his words and push the other thoughts out. But something inside my head won't cooperate. His tone is authoritative and confident, making even this simple instruction sound like a preface to a seduction … at least from where I'm standing. But of course, he isn't considering anything of the sort. I push him away.

"I got it. I don't need the McGuire tutorial on how to stand."

He chuckles. "Okay. Then show me, hot stuff. Throw it."

I look down the field at Hayley. *Oh shit.*

She cups her hand around her mouth and shouts, "Come on, Ragan."

Disregarding everything Branch told me, I throw the ball to Hayley and this time it soars in her general direction just enough for her to shift right and catch it.

I look over at Branch. "See. I don't need any of your fancy football techniques. Now let's get this over with. I have an early shift tomorrow and I'm already tired."

Thanks to my disregard for Branch's advice, we lose the game, but Branch's fans and the crowd eat up every minute of the embarrassment that's the Annual Blue Ridge Bowl.

"You should learn to listen to those who are wiser than you."

I look up at him with a scowl. "Blow me."

"Just tell me when, sugar."

STAY CONNECTED WITH LILLY

Facebook Fan Page
www.facebook.com/authorlillywilde

Facebook Reader Group
www.facebook.com/groups/TheWildeLillies

Instagram
www.instagram.com/authorlillywilde

Twitter
twitter.com/authorlilly

Goodreads
www.goodreads.com/author/show/8577407.Lilly_Wilde

Google+
plus.google.com/115013089578343874604

LinkedIn
www.linkedin.com/in/lillywilde

YouTube
www.youtube.com/channel/UCyzbRGz2o-pIRMDq0ncw3Jw

Pinterest
www.pinterest.com/lillywilde

Thank you for reading **Shattered Beginnings**. If you enjoyed it, I would love to hear from you! Please take a moment to leave a review at your favorite retailer. Thanks!

Would you like to be a part of Lilly's upcoming book releases? Sign up to be a member of her launch team.

ABOUT THE AUTHOR

Lilly Wilde is a wife and mom who loves to fill each day with happiness and laughter. Lilly loves to dream, get lost in fantasy, and create alternate worlds in which we can escape ever so often. She's down-to-earth, engaging, and compassionate, with a great sense of humor. Her laughter is one of the first qualities that you'll notice; you'll become instantly drawn to her witty and fun-loving spirit.

Lilly spent a lot of time daydreaming as a child, which led to numerous hours of reading and eventually the writing of poetry. After years of starting and stopping several novels, she eventually set a goal to complete her debut novel, Untouched.

Her stories are of strength, growth, facing demons, and stepping outside your comfort zone. They often surround topics of family and love and the beauty of both.